I'VE BEEN WAITING

WAITING

D1354344

WILLIAM L HARBEN

Fulton Books
Meadville, PA

Published by Fulton Books 2023

ISBN 978-1-63985-167-6 (paperback)
ISBN 978-1-63985-168-3 (digital)

Printed in the United States of America

CHAPTER 1

As the sun began to settle, John found himself in an unfamiliar area. Dark shadows began to appear everywhere with each passing moment as the sun descended lower and lower behind the tree-tops. The woods were quickly filling with dark, hazy, uncomfortable images that seemed to come to life, surrounding him in all directions. Feeling uneasy, John just wanted to find his family as soon as possible and get out of there. *Where are they?* he thought.

Suddenly, he heard the crying screams of his family from a distance not far away. His son and daughter, almost at the same moment, yelled out, "Daddy! Daddy!" This was followed by his wife's screams, "John! We're over here."

As he turned to scour the area with what little light he had left, he noticed a group of men standing in a small clearing. They began laughing as they looked down while passing around a bottle of whiskey, each taking a sip before passing it on to the other. Again, he heard the crying voices of his family. Only this time, his wife was pleading, "No. Please don't do this. My family has done nothing to you. Please let us go!"

The men began laughing louder, giving them a sense of pleasure as they dominated over their victims. Filled with a desperate rage, John began hurrying over to save his family, but his legs were heavy. The harder he tried to run, the heavier they became. It was like running through a pool of thick mud. Finally, John got to within fifteen yards of the clearing. He noticed that the group of men were nowhere in sight and that his family had been tied together. They were sitting on the ground in a small circle around the flickering light of the nearby campfire. He realized that this was his chance. So without delay, he leaped over a large damp log and ran up to his family. They were elated to see him, and for the time being, John could see the relief in his family's faces. His wife, son, and young daughter were all there.

"Shush. Keep quiet. We must hurry!" John said. He quickly untied the three, and they hurried off to the darkness near the edge of the clearing. Without saying a word, they all hugged one another before disappearing into the woods. It wasn't long when an unfamiliar voice echoed through the night air.

"Hey. They're gone! Quickly, everyone, spread out. They couldn't have gotten far."

John's daughter let out a scream as she tripped over some dark hidden object on the ground. They could hear the voices.

"Over here. They're over here!"

"Well, go get 'em!" another yelled out.

John's family hurried through the woods. All were holding hands as they desperately tried to make their way through the dark night in hopes of reaching their car. They could sense that the men were close behind, chasing and getting closer with every step. Suddenly, the ground started to become luminescent as they realized that the men were gaining on them and now had them in the sights of their flashlights. Somehow through the darkness, John spotted his car. It wasn't far. "Hurry, just a little farther," he said.

As they arrived at the car, his family quickly went to their assigned doors and waited as John reached into his pocket to get his keys. In his panic, however, John fumbled the keys on the ground. A moment later, four men stepped out of the woods and stood in front of the car. Their flashlights were blinding, and all that could be heard was their intimidating laughter coming from the four men. His family was frozen in fear while their hearts were pounding in their chests as they waited for what might happen next. No one was speaking but just staring. The intense quiet was unusual to the point that it seemed deafening. Then a strong low-pitched evil-sounding voice that penetrated the night air said, "Now we got ya!" followed by a chilling silence. Then the cocking of guns as the men prepared to fire their weapons. John screamed out, "No!" as the weapons flashed.

A violent shaking took over John's senses. As he woke, he realized that he'd had another nightmare.

His wife, in her soft voice, asked, "Honey are you all right?"

John, disoriented and in a cold sweat, replied, "Yeah, I'm okay. Just another bad dream."

He took a deep breath and then slowly rolled over to hold his wife, holding her tightly.

As John fell back to sleep, Eve, his wife, slowly eased out of bed so as not to wake her troubled husband. She went to the family study to remove a journal that she had kept hidden in the back of a drawer in her desk. She quietly opened the journal and wrote, "October 1. Another nightmare." She then flipped back through the pages and noted that his nightmares were becoming more frequent and more intense. Then suddenly, she heard the soft voice of her eight-year-old daughter.

"Mommy, I'm hungry," she said as she scratched her eyes.

"Yes, I know. I'll fix breakfast in a bit. Why don't you go wake up your brother? He has a big game today, and he needs to start getting ready."

"Okay," she said, and off she went.

Eve smiled as she watched her daughter hurry off. Then she turned back to the journal. Her smile disappeared, and the look of concern took over her expression. "It's time. This has gone on long enough." She reached down and grabbed her address book. In it was the address and phone number of a long dear friend. She was a psychiatrist. *If anyone can help, she can. I'll call her when we get back from the game*, she thought.

She put her books away for safekeeping and went to the kitchen to begin making everyone's favorite breakfast—French toast. It wasn't long before the aroma drifted throughout the house as if to call everyone to the breakfast table. They all exchanged good mornings, a quick prayer, and then began to eat.

"Well, I hope everyone had sweet dreams last night," asked Eve.

John lifted his eyes and looked at his wife from across the table. He could see the concern written on her face, but neither wanted to let on to the other that they were worried.

At almost the same time, their children responded, "I did. I did."

"That's great. Some say that our dreams can tell us things about ourselves," responded Eve.

"Like what, Mommy?" their daughter asked.

"Oh, some say that our dreams are trying to tell us of things that may someday really happen to us. It could be good or it could be telling us to be careful. But most of the time, they are simply fun adventures that we experience as we sleep."

"Well, I had a dream that you were making sugar cookies and that I was helping. Then we took them to cheerleading practice, and Cindy, our head cheerleader, ate them all. She got so full and big that she couldn't fit into her cheerleading uniform and had to quit cheerleading. That's when I was named the new head cheerleader. What does that dream mean? Do you think that could really happen?" their daughter asked.

Everyone had a big laugh as no one knew exactly what to tell her. The family finished eating. Then they began preparing for the big game. John's son was the star running back on his football team. Each Saturday, the family had the same ritualistic routine. They would first eat and then all would get dressed. John and his son would then spend about thirty minutes playing catch in the backyard before heading out to the game. It was something that John and his son had done for years. The bond that he had with his son was unique, and the strong love that they all had for one another made them a family that all who knew them would admire.

It turned out to be a cool fall Saturday morning in Boston. All the parents were out, watching their sons compete in little league football. Only ten years of age, John's son was an accomplished young athlete. All that watched him play marveled at his athletic abilities. As John sat in the stands, watching and admiring his son's achievements, he realized how very proud he was of his family. While his son played football, his daughter, who was only eight years old, was one of the team's cheerleaders. It seemed she had a calling of her own. And, of course, John's wife, Eve, was right beside her. She was the typical cheerleader mom, making sure that everyone was having fun. She was as dedicated as any mother, giving full support to all her children's activities. As John sat looking down from the bleachers, he thought to himself, *What a perfect family. Could I ever imagine having such a perfect life and family?* With that, he smiled; and with that smile, he also wondered what he would do if anything were to ever happen to any of them. He knew that he would be shattered.

John worked as a narcotics agent and had always been aware of the dangers of his occupation. He had always tried to keep his family out of harm's way. However, lately, he had been suffering from recurring nightmares that had resulted in his family being violently and horrifically attacked. He had tried to keep this from his family because he didn't want to create any worry. So he had kept this to himself. However, as of late, these nightmares had been occurring more frequently than usual, and he knew that his wife was beginning to raise questions about his ongoing bad dreams. They were becoming so disturbing to John that much of his time at work was spent making sure that he didn't put himself in a position that would threaten his family.

Suddenly, his pager went off. He knew what that meant. Unfortunately, he would have to leave the game because there might be a break in the case he was currently working on. John waved to his wife as he walked down from the bleachers. She looked up and waved back. She knew as well that he had to go. And each time he left, she didn't know if he would be coming back. They both had an unspoken understanding about his job and the dangers involved. She would not dare suggest to John that he should think about another career because she knew how much he loved his job. So she quietly accepted the career that he had chosen and tried not to think about the dangers that might someday take her husband.

As John got in his car, he immediately called his partner on his cell phone. His partner's name was

Dexter. He called him Dex for short. Dex was just getting started in law enforcement. Why he chose law enforcement is anybody's guess because he was such a naturally nervous person. It just didn't seem to fit his demeanor. When Dex got nervous or excited about something, he began to stutter terribly. He'd had this problem since childhood. No one really thought that Dex would last very long in law enforcement because of his nervousness. In fact, John originally partnered with Dex to protect him.

However, one thing that was amazing about Dex was his uncanny ability to come up with relevant information about a case. In many instances, he had been able to provide critical information through his research and contacts that had been instrumental in solving a case. Even though Dex had proven his worth time and time again, no one knew how long he would last in this type of highly stressful work.

If that wasn't bad enough, trying to talk to Dex on the phone was an adventure in itself because of his stuttering problem. It seemed to really get bad when he had big news about an ongoing case like this one. The two men had been working on a case that involved a well-established smuggling ring. The ring had mob connections and was smuggling crack cocaine into the Boston area. As Dex answered the phone, John could sense that Dex was extremely excited about something. He was so excited that he could hardly speak.

"Ja-Ja-John? I-I-Is that you?" Dex asked.

"Yes, Dex, it's me. Just calm down, take a deep breath, and tell me what you have."

"O-O-Okay," said Dex. "I na-na-know wa-wa-where they're m-m-meeting and th-th-they're meeting tonight. I-In fact, th-th-they're making an e-e-exchange."

An exchange was a key word that John and Dex used when there was a load of drugs coming into a drop sight. Usually, the buyer would have prearranged for the money to be there at the time of the drop. It would be a stroke of luck if they were able to determine just where a drop was going to take place before it actually happened.

John asked Dex, "Are you sure about this? You know where they're going to make an exchange?" Before Dex could answer, John said, "Wait. Don't answer that, Dex. Just keep quiet for now. I will meet you at our usual place."

John hung up the phone and headed toward their meeting place, which was a little coffee shop. It was located on a street corner. The perfect location, which allowed for the fresh aroma of coffee to drift down the streets in every direction. As a coffee lover, one could appreciate their perfection in brewing coffee. In fact, they were known to all coffee-drinking connoisseurs in the Boston community. Anytime the two men had something to discuss such as a case, they knew that this was the place to meet.

What John didn't realize was that his life would be changing after this day and that his worst nightmares about his family's well-being were beginning to be set into place. Nothing he could do from this time forward would be able to change the outcome that he so feared.

CHAPTER 2

John felt guilty as he drove off to meet Dex. He knew this must be an important lead for Dex to have called him away from his son's Saturday morning game. Dex knew how much John loved to watch his son compete in athletics.

As John drove up to the little corner coffee shop, he noticed Dex looking somewhat nervous and very impatient more so than usual. As he parked his car, John began to get an uneasy feeling in his gut. Maybe it was that instinctive feeling that he would sometimes get when things were not right.

He stepped out of his car and cautiously walked toward Dex who began to move away from the front door of the coffee shop, motioning for John to follow. John, feeling this to be a bit odd, realized that Dex might be in some sort of trouble. He quickly reached into his jacket to make sure he had his revolver. Dex then motioned to John again to follow as he moved around the corner and out of John's field of view. John, with his hand in his coat and firmly on his revolver, began to ease around the corner using extreme caution. He noticed Dex standing alongside a black Cadillac with two men sitting inside. Dex looked at John and again motioned, saying, "J-J-John, ca-ca-come on over."

John, feeling somewhat nervous himself, began to move toward the car. As he approached, he realized that there were two men in the car. They worked for a boss named Jimmy and were part of the organization that they had been investigating. These two had a vicious reputation, and John knew immediately that this was not a good situation. As he approached, he looked at Dex as if he was asking him if he was all right. Dex looked back at John, looking as nervous as ever but letting John know that he was all right for the time being.

Anticipating the worst to happen, John leaned over and peered into the car, saying, "Boys, what can we do for ya today?" The two men turned to John, allowing him to get a better look. He realized that the driver was a kid named Telly, a youngster who was trying to work his way up in the organization. No one knew a lot about this kid other than he had a reputation of liking to play with fire. The other guy in the car was Nick. His street name was Nick the Hammer. He was about as mean as they come. Rumor had it that he liked to use a hammer on people who had fallen out of Jimmy's good standings.

Nick then responded to John by saying, "Jimmy wants us to deliver a personal message."

"What would that be?" asked John.

"Jimmy wants you two guys to back off before something happens to someone you hold dear to your heart if you know what we mean," said Nick as he and Telly began to smirk.

John, not knowing exactly how to respond, tried to mislead the two. However, he wanted to know what these two were up to.

John laughed and said, "Come on, guys. We are here to have a cup of coffee between friends. Would you like to join us? You can tell me more about this guy named Jimmy you keep referring to."

Dex then began to elaborate by saying, "Ya-ya-yes, th-th-that's right. Wa-wa—"

Before Dex could finish, he was rudely cut off by Nick the Hammer. John and Dex could tell he was becoming agitated when he replied with a more serious tone in his voice.

"Dex!" he shouted. "Shut up. Until you can learn to talk, don't, especially when I'm around. That really bugs me." He then directed his attention toward John. "Now look! You two need to back off. You know what we are talking about, so don't make the mistake and try to play dumb. This is your only warning. Next time, we won't be so nice if you know what I mean, and I think you do." With that, the two men started their car and hurriedly drove away.

John and Dex just stood there. They were both startled by the unexpected event.

He looked over at Dex, smiled, and said, "Well, we must be getting close to something. For Jimmy to feel that he needed to attempt to scare us off only means that they're starting to get nervous. We must be on to something."

"I th-th-think so," said Dex. "I f-f-found out about a-a-an e-exchange tonight. Th-th-that's why I ca-ca-called you s-s-so w-we could meet here and d-d-discuss this."

John began to get very excited about hearing the news of a possible exchange. Without giving much thought to the warning that they had just received from Nick and Telly, the two men decided to go inside for some coffee and discuss what Dex had heard about the exchange.

Dex told John that the exchange was scheduled at 1:30 a.m. at the shipping yards near dock number thirteen. Upon hearing this, John became curious as to how Dex had come across this information. He wondered to himself if he was being set up. It just seemed too easy. He also knew how careful these guys had been in the past, and with this unexpected encounter, he wasn't so sure.

"So, Dex, how did you come across this information?" asked John.

Dex said, "I w-w-was contacted b-b-by R-R-Ricky Baitmen. I-I-I've known him s-s-since junior high."

"Is he reliable?" asked John. Dex nodded. "Okay, so how does he get his information?"

"He w-w-works at the d-d-docks, and he o-o-overheard a conversation b-b-between his boss and a tr-tr-trucker," replied Dex.

With that, the two men decided that they had to follow up on this lead. They called in their support team and decided to prepare for a long night at the docks. To be able to catch these guys making an actual drop would be too good to be true.

As they gathered their team, John laid out the plan so that everyone would understand what was expected. They made sure that they had all the necessary items that they would need to make a good arrest. John and Dex were excited yet nervous and knew this could be the break that they needed to put Jimmy and his smuggling operation away for a very long time.

While they were preparing for a long night at the docks and hoping that this was a good lead, John began to wonder to himself if this was going to be another wasted night like so many in the past. He began to think about his family and how he wished he could have seen his son play football today. He wanted to watch his daughter cheer on the sidelines with his wife close by her side. He wished he could be with them tonight with his wife and family, simply spending time together and enjoying a quiet evening.

However, like so many times in the past, John would be out somewhere in the night, doing his job and putting his life on the line. John and his team pulled into the area. They moved in slowly, careful to keep their distance so as not to warn any suspicious characters. The key to a successful stakeout was to keep everything as it is. Nothing should be out of place. Nothing new or unusual should be in view. His team of men were professionals with years of experience, and they knew how to do their jobs. The men unloaded from their vehicles and quietly gathered for last-minute instruction.

Suddenly, a strong unexplainable, uneasy feeling came over John as the strong stench of dead fish filled the night air. John hesitated, looked around, and composed himself before addressing his team. "A trap has been set tonight, fellows," John said. "So let's prepare ourselves for a long night. Be careful and wait for my signal before anyone moves in. We do this right, then we can finally get these guys and their dope off our streets." Everyone nodded that they understood and took their positions as the waiting began. John was right. A trap had been set. But for whom?

CHAPTER 3

It was an extremely dark evening, the air heavy with moisture from an incoming fog. They could hear the sound of a far-off bell ringing or banging in the distance. It seemed to be the only sound that could be heard at the docks that night. The normal squawks and flutters of seagulls that were usually present at the docks could neither be heard. The uneasy silence seemed to echo a predestined warning that all was not right on this dark evening. Each man could hear their own heart pounding in their chests with the anticipation of what was about to happen. These situations were never easy, and knowing that they could be killed at any moment made it even that much more intense. There was one small hazy light located above dock door number thirteen. It seemed to provide the men with the only light by which they could see.

Everyone was in place. Each corner of the building, front and back, was being watched. The officers had been trained for these things and were professionally prepared to do their jobs. They waited quietly, not making a sound or movement that might give away their position. As the nighttime hours passed, and the evening began to slip into the early morning. The officers began wondering if this was just another wasted night with another false lead.

It was about 3:00 a.m. All the officers were becoming disappointed, tired, and frustrated. Their patience had almost run out when what looked like a white truck pulled up and parked near the dock door. John and the other officers became aroused with excitement as they focused on the truck and waited nervously to see what might happen next. Suddenly, the truck door opened, and an individual stepped out. He looked around and then placed something under the windshield wiper of the truck. He then looked around for a second time and quickly walked away, disappearing into the fog. No one felt that it was time to move in, so everyone held his position, waiting for something else to happen. But nothing did.

It was around 5:30 a.m., and John decided that they had waited long enough. He signaled for the officers to begin moving in on the premises. One of the officers immediately moved up to the truck and after checking the windshield, noticed a note had been left for the officers to find. The officer radioed over to John, saying, "John, you need to get down here!" After securing the grounds and discovering that there was no one in or around the area, all the officers merged around the truck.

John asked the officer who had radioed, "What is it? What do you have?"

"It's a note. It has your name on it," the officer said.

John took the note from the officer and began to open it. The other officers made their way to the rear of the truck to see what was inside. The note simply read, "WE WARNED YOU!" Upon reading those words, John felt the blood rush from his head, and his heart began to beat rapidly as he felt a sinking feeling in his gut. He had an overwhelming feeling that his family was in immediate danger. Just then, one of the officers yelled for John to come to the rear of the truck.

He heard one of the officers ask, "Does anybody know this guy?" John and Dex stepped inside the rear of the truck.

Dex looked at John and said, "Th-th-that's Baitmen. R-R-Ricky B-B-Baitmen. He's the guy who t-t-told me about this e-e-exchange."

Ricky had been tied to a chair and shot in the back of the head, execution-style. John immediately knew he had been set up, and he knew he had to get back to his family as soon as possible. He picked up his radio and called headquarters. With a nervous and somewhat panicky tone, he said, "I need someone to get to my house immediately and make sure my family is safe. I-I'll meet you there. Also, send an ambulance to the waterfronts dock number thirteen." John then told Dex to stay at the docks and search through everything. "Try to find out something, anything, to tie Jimmy and his boys to this," he said. "I've got to go home and check on my family.

I need to know that they're okay." John took a deep breath as a worried look took over his expression. "I will call you later," he added. With that, John hurried to his car and sped away.

John was shaken by the note and knew that he had to hurry. He drove in a panic to get back to his family as he felt that sinking feeling in his gut. It was a feeling that was hard to describe, but it was a feeling of helplessness and high anxiety.

John knew that as long as the dispatch operator didn't call him and his radio remained silent, his family was most likely safe. At the same time, he was hoping that he was simply exaggerating his worry and that his wife and children were safely tucked in their beds fast asleep.

As he drove, he noticed that his cell phone was showing a message on his voice mail. He never realized a call had come in because he had turned off the ringer during their stakeout at the docks. He picked up his phone and dialed in to check his message.

The call had come in around 9:00 p.m. from the night before. It was his wife and kids, each leaving him a message. They said, "Daddy, we hope you're okay. We decided to order pizza and wanted to leave you a message. We love you. Good night, and we will see you in the morning."

As John hung up the phone, his eyes began to tear up with emotion. It seemed that everything was happening so fast. Yet for him, he felt like he was moving in slow motion. He was about halfway home. It was around 6:00 a.m., barely thirty minutes had passed since they went down to check out the white truck.

John decided to go ahead and call his wife from his cell phone. He reached down, dialed the phone, and it started to ring. No answer. He waited, and the phone continued to ring. Still, no answer. John thought to himself, *Okay, maybe no one is awake. It is awfully early*. But the phone continued to ring. By now, he thought somebody should have answered. He said out loud in a frantic tone, "Come on, Eve, answer the phone. Let me know you're all okay."

A moment later, a voice came over the radio. It was the dispatch operator in a soft, delicate, and shaken voice. She said, "John. John, can you pick up?" John tossed the cell phone down and just stared at the radio. Then he heard her voice again. The way she sounded, he knew something wasn't right. All he could do was stare down at the radio, trembling and frozen with the fear that his worst nightmare may be true.

Then she asked again, "John, can you hear me? Please pick up."

He took a deep breath, reached over, and picked up the radio, "I'm here, Shelly."

Shelly said, "John," followed by a long pause. Then she said again, "John, where are you?"

"I'm about twenty minutes from my house."

She said, "John, you need to come to the office."

"What is it, Shelly? I'm only twenty minutes from my house. I need to be home," he replied.

"I'm so sorry, John! We got there as soon as we could, but we were too late. There was nothing anyone could do. Please come to the office."

Upon hearing those words from Shelly, he became numb. A blank stare came over his face as he continued to drive toward home. He knew he had to be there. *Maybe they were wrong*, he thought to himself. He threw down the radio that he had been clutching in his hand as he pulled up to the house. There were police cars, fire trucks, and several ambulances parked in his front yard. He got out of his car and stood there, watching in shock. Everyone was frantically scrambling about, trying to do what they could to save what was left of the house.

Chief Woodrow, John's boss, noticed that John had arrived at the scene. He immediately went over to John in hopes that he could offer some sort of condolences. But what does one say at a time like this? He wanted John to know that he was there for him and to make sure he wasn't going to do anything irrational, like running into the house. To his amazement, John was relatively calm. He just stood there watching, not saying a word. Chief Woodrow said, "John. John." But there was no response. "John, come go with me. You need to sit down." John didn't reply or even acknowledge that the chief had said anything. He then began to make his way over to the ambulances that were parked in his yard. There were three, one for each.

CHAPTER 4

Three days had passed since the funerals of his family members. John was still in a trancelike state, like he had entered into a new world, a world that seemed to turn John into a cold and hardened individual with one goal: to relentlessly hunt down those responsible for the deaths of his family. This new world became John's tortured reality—that his family was no longer a part of his life. In this new world, there was no escape from the personal and private pain that he constantly endured as he envisioned his wife and young children lying in their coffins. He realized that he would not see his children grow up and succeed. He would no longer be able to cheer for his children while he watched from the sidelines. And he wouldn't be able to grow old with his wife or hold her in his arms again.

With each day that passed, John's heart hardened. All he could think about was getting revenge on the individuals who did this. Filled with self-pity and anger, he began to drink heavily, trying to numb his senses from the pain that was beginning to consume his life. He isolated himself in a small, dark, and dungy apartment near a corner bar. Ignoring phone calls and messages from personal friends, he had no need for pleasantries. He cut off all communications with those people who cared most for him, including his partner, Dex. John left his isolation only to retrieve some beer and food to simply survive. He realized that what he had to do, he had to do alone and that no one would be able to help him achieve his ultimate goal of revenge.

So after about two weeks of isolation and torment, he began to get his thoughts together and formulate a plan. John knew that he would be breaking the laws that he had worked so hard to uphold and that his style of justice could cost him his life or his freedom. But he felt that he had nothing to live for if he couldn't share his life with his family.

First, however, he had to resign his position at the police force so he could begin his pursuit of these people. Therefore, he went to police headquarters, and without warning or explanation, he turned in his letter of resignation. Chief Woodrow, noticing that John was in the station, called for him to come into his office and shut the door.

He said, "John, we've been worried about you. No one has been able to reach you. You won't return any phone calls." John had no reply or response to what the chief had just said. He simply sat there with a blank stare on his face, looking out of the office window. Chief Woodrow noticed that John's appearance reflected a person who was in serious emotional trouble. He noticed that John hadn't shaved in some time and that he was beginning to look extremely scruffy. He also had dark circles under his eyes and stringy hair that looked as though it hadn't been combed or washed in quite a while.

"John, I'm really concerned. As a friend, I wish I knew what to do or say, but I don't," said the chief. John still had nothing to say. The door opened, and the chief's secretary came into the room, handing a note for the chief.

Chief Woodrow read it, then looked at John and said, "Now wait a minute. You're not serious about resigning. If you need an extended amount of time, no problem. Take as long as you need. We all understand what you must be going through."

With that, John quickly looked into Chief Woodrow's eyes, and with an angry yet shaken tone in his voice, he said, "You have NO idea!"

He then stood up, handed the chief his badge and his gun, and without saying another word, he turned and left.

As John left, he decided to go by his old house and try to locate any of his old guns. He was hoping that they had survived the fire without damage since he had stored them in a safe. He pulled up to the house and got out of the car carrying a black athletic bag.

As he made his way through the house, his eyes filled with emotion. Each room that he entered brought back a flood of memories that were almost too much to bear, but he continued onward. After stumbling through most of the house, he finally made his way to his bedroom. John just stood there looking. It became difficult for him to go forward because his room was where they found the bodies of his family. They were all in bed, lying there together as they had so many times when John was out all night on a stakeout. He began to sob uncontrollably.

Finally, he found the strength to go to the closet where he kept his guns. The safe was in the closet, and he hoped that it hadn't burned up or been taken by the authorities. As he entered the closet, he noticed that his wife's clothes had fallen off the racks and were slightly burned. The smell of smoke and toxins was almost overwhelming. He moved a pile of clothes away from the corner of the closet where he knew that his safe was supposed to be. To his surprise, the safe was still there.

He bent down and opened it, and there were his guns. He quickly gathered them and placed them in his athletic bag, but he also noticed a black metal box that he had never realized was there before. In it were photos of his family that Eve had accumulated through the years. There were keepsakes of all sorts, birth certificates, their marriage license, and other items that she felt were important to their memories. He thought about how fortunate he was to have come across this and packed it away as well. Then he began to make his way back to the car.

As he drove away from the burned house, he knew he was closing off a part of his life that he could never reclaim. However, finding that box of memories provided John with a deeper motivation to do what he had to do. He was more determined than ever to find those people who were responsible if it was the last thing he ever did, and he knew who to go after first.

John decided that dock 13 might be the best place to start, so he drove there, parked his car, and waited. He wasn't exactly sure what he was going to do, but he decided to wait until dark. He thought that he could sneak into the building and maybe come across some names and addresses. John was particularly interested in locating an address for Nick and Telly. He was in the same observation place as the night of the stakeout, a secluded brushy area across the street from the door. This time, however, he had the advantage for they didn't know he would be there.

It was about 6:15 p.m. when the employees made their way to their cars and were leaving for home. John noticed that there was one car left in the parking area, and he thought this would be a good time to slip in and ask this guy some questions. Not knowing what he might find once inside or who it was that was still there, John thought that he should be prepared for the worst.

He entered the building as quietly and cautiously as possible with gun in hand. Immediately, his eyes focused on a small office in a corner near the front door. The office had glass walls with mini blinds that had been pulled down, but they were open just enough to allow John to see inside. As he looked through the blinds, he noticed that there was someone sitting behind a desk doing some sort of paperwork.

John put his gun behind his back and walked into the room without making a noise or saying a word. He stood there quietly, waiting for the man to look up. It seemed as though ten minutes had passed before he finally looked up.

As the man looked up at John, his eyes opened wide with surprise, and he began to get very nervous. John realized from his reaction that this man, whoever he was, knew John and probably knew something about what had happened with his family. As the man began to scurry about, John got concerned that he would pull a gun out of a drawer somewhere.

"Wait a minute. Just relax. Put your hands on top of the table real slow where I can see them," John said as he pulled out his gun and carefully aimed at the man.

"Sure, no problem," the man said as he looked around the room.

John stood there looking at the man when he realized that he was the guy who pulled up and parked the white truck the night at the stakeout.

"Hey, aren't you the guy who left that note on the truck the other night?" he asked.

"No. No, I mean, what truck? What are you talking about?" the man asked.

"I need a name," asked John with an angry tone.

"A name. What name?" the man asked with a sarcastic-yet-nervous laugh.

John then cocked his gun and stuck it to the man's forehead, saying, "Look, I got something you want, and you have something I want." That sarcastic grin immediately left the man's face as sweat beads began to form on the man's forehead. "What do you have that I need?" he asked. John, demonstrating his own composed and sarcastic grin, said, "YOUR FINGERS."

Upon hearing that, the man jumped up and tried to fight his way out of the situation, but John, wasting no time, hit the man over his head with his gun—knocking him to the floor.

As the man came to, he found himself tied to a chair with his hands placed on top of the table and secured with a heavy wrapping of duct tape. He was unable to move with the exception of his fingers, which were left unwrapped and in full view. Being at the fishing docks where fish were processed and packaged on a daily basis made it easy for John to find the necessary items he would need to get information out of this guy.

"Now I'm going to ask you one more time before you start losing fingers," John said. "I need the names of the people who slaughtered my family."

The man was shaken up and began looking around as if he thought someone was going to help him. As he began to sweat profusely, he looked at John, took a big gulp, and said with a soft nervous voice, "I'm sorry. I don't know what you're talking about."

"Wrong answer!" shouted John.

He then pulled out a huge meat cleaver that he had found in the fish processing area. With no hesitation, John slammed it down on the man's right hand, quickly and completely severing all four of the man's fingers. The man let out a blood-curdling scream as he passed out.

About ten minutes had passed before the man regained consciousness. He looked down at his right hand and was shocked to find all his fingers were missing except his thumb.

He was trembling and soaked with sweat when he looked at John and said with a shaken voice, "I didn't think you'd do it!"

"Oh yeah, I'm going to take the next four and then I'm going to move right up your arm until you tell me what I want," John said.

John began to get this crazed look about him as he paced back and forth in front of the man. The man watched John as he was becoming more and more enraged.

Leaning over the table, John said with a more violent tone, "Now who are they?" as he raised the cleaver for a second time.

"No, wait. Wait!" the man shouted. "Okay, I'll tell you what you want." He caught his breath and began to tell John that he was approached by Telly and Nick. "They asked me to drive that white truck and park it in front by the door under the light. They said to pull up around 3:00 a.m., leave this note on the windshield, and walk away. Knowing Nick and Telly, well, you don't ask why. You just do it."

"Where are they now?" asked John.

"I don't know," he replied. John then raised the cleaver again. "Okay. Okay, they stay at a fishing cabin."

"What fishing cabin? Where?" John shouted.

"They are hiding out at Jimmy's lake house on Mystic Lake on the southwest side."

"How will I find it?" asked John.

"You will find it. There are only a couple of cabins out there. This one has a metal gate entrance with a rocking J over the centerpiece."

John smiled. "Okay. Now wasn't that easy? All this unnecessary pain could have been avoided," he said as he turned and began to walk toward the door.

"Hey, wait a minute. What about me? You're not going to just leave me here like this, are you? I need a doctor!" the man shouted.

John kept moving toward the door as if he were ignoring the man. As John reached the door, he turned, looked at the man, and said, "A doctor. Why do you think you need a doctor?"

"Because of my hand. Look at what you did. Man, you gotta get me a doctor or untie me so I can go!" he shouted. John quickly pointed his gun and fired, hitting the man in the center of his forehead.

As he slumped down silently in the chair, John said in a soft voice, "Go! You can go all right, straight to HELL."

He stared at the man as the blood from his wound began filling the tabletop. An uneasy feeling came over him as he realized that he had now crossed the line and that there was no turning back. Then slowly, he reached into his pocket and pulled out the note that had been left on the truck, the night of the stakeout. He unfolded it and laid it on the table between the dead man's hands. He then pinned it on the table by sticking the cleaver through it. John wanted Jimmy and his boys to know who did this and that the rules had changed.

CHAPTER 5

John knew that it wouldn't be long before Jimmy and some of his men discovered the man's body. He wasn't worried about the authorities because he knew that that was the last thing that Jimmy needed. He would probably dispose of the body within the organization and try to handle this internally.

However, John knew that he had to be more careful because Jimmy would soon be aware that John was only looking for revenge and not legal justice. That should worry Jimmy more than anything. He also knew that he would still have the advantage until the body was discovered and word got out within the organization.

John had no time to waste in pursuit of Telly and Nick, so he headed straight out to the lake. He was hoping that he could find the two relaxed and off guard, but still, he knew he had to be careful because these two were the worst of the worst when it came to being vicious.

It took John about two hours to get to the lake. It was late, and John was tired and hungry, so he stopped at an old log cabin-style convenience store on his way into the lake area. The store owner was on hand and excited to see someone come in. He seemed to be a friendly old coot and appeared to be about eighty years old. He looked as though he had spent most of his youth in the sun fishing from the looks of his prune-like dried skin. He was also suffering from a bad case of hearing loss.

As John walked into the store, the old man said with a smile, revealing his missing front teeth, "How ya doing?" John just grinned and nodded, still not feeling very social and trying to keep a low profile. He moved about the store, gathering up a few items that he felt might satisfy his hunger while taking an occasional glance at the old man.

The old man seemed to be focused on John's every move, which made John a bit nervous. He noticed that the old man was standing there with this eerie toothless grin on his face. John saw a map of the lake, which he promptly picked up. Then he began looking for his favorite snack, which was fried cherry pies.

However, he couldn't find any of these fried delights, and feeling somewhat annoyed, he asked the old man, "Hey, old man, you got any fried pies?"

"Ey, what ya say?" asked the old man.

Realizing that the old man had a hearing problem, John asked in a slower and louder tone, "You got any fried pies?"

"A fried eye. Son, what and the heck are you going to catch out here with a fried eye? I've got some livers, gizzards, and some shrimp in the freezer box but no fried eyes."

"No. No, not a fried eye. A fried pie?"

"A tired pie. Well, son, my pie tired out a long time ago. Real shame, too, if you know what I mean."

John began to laugh. For the first time in a long time, he actually laughed. It felt good for a brief moment, and a spark of life resurfaced in his eyes. Just as suddenly, he stopped.

"Never mind. Just forget it."

John took his stuff to the checkout counter where the old man was waiting. As John piled up his stuff on the counter, the old man began to talk again.

"Here fer some fishen?" he asked.

"No, just passing through," replied John as he took out some money from his pocket.

"Well, it's always good to relax," the old man said.

John smiled and said in a softer tone, "Yeah, I know what you mean!"

"Ey, what you say?" the old man asked.

"I said I got this map too!" John said as he shook his head.

"Okay. Okay, no need to get cranky. By the way, you know, you look like you've had some trouble." John just stood there exchanging eye contact with the old man—not answering or responding to his last statement. They stood there looking at each other as the old man began to elaborate, "Son, we all got trouble, some worse than others. But it's the way we handle those troubles. That's what's important. What you do next, it's all up to you and that's what you have to live with."

Feeling somewhat shocked by what the old man had said, he pulled out ten dollars and threw it on the counter, saying, "Here. Keep the change."

As John gathered up his stuff from the counter, he began having an eerie feeling as he looked at the old man. It was as though the old man had turned into someone else right before his eyes. He suddenly had this serious look on his face—no smile, no emotion. He just stood there staring at John. Feeling uncomfortable and anxious to leave, John said in a troubled tone, "Old man, you need some help!" With no reply, the old man began to grin again, showing off his lack of teeth, which gave John an even more uncomfortable feeling.

John drove off as quickly as he could while absorbing what had just occurred. He had this uneasy, strange feeling after his conversation with the old man. *Maybe I just need to get some food down*, he thought to himself.

After driving far enough from the store that he began to feel comfortable again, he pulled over on the shoulder of the road. He ate his food while checking the map. It was about nine thirty at night and extremely dark. Being near the lake, there were no lights for miles. The dark clouds in the night sky prevented any light of the moon from shining through. It was about as dark as it could possibly be. John thought this was a perfect night to do what he had to do. He just hoped he could get out here and do this before any of Jimmy's men warned them.

As he sat in the car looking at the map, he was trying to determine the main roads that traveled around the lake. After determining his best route, he started to drive. John began to think about the old man at the store, *What was that about*, he wondered? *Surely, he wasn't trying to give me advice or tell me something. He doesn't know anything about me.*

He continued to drive along the dark winding roads. His mind was troubled, thinking about the old man. Suddenly, he drove around a hairpin turn and saw a metal gate with a rocking J at the top. "This is it," he said to himself. He drove past and turned into a dirt road about a quarter of a mile from the gate. "Perfect," he said to himself.

John got out of his car and looked around, taking in the sounds and fragrances of the night. The smells of nature, the pine trees, wild grasses, and the sounds of the night wildlife made for a peaceful and relaxed setting.

It would inspire any nature lover to consider moving to the country. He thought what a shame to spoil all this with what he had to do tonight. But he was here to do one thing and that was to get even with Telly and Nick for destroying his family and the perfect world that he once enjoyed.

He began to walk toward the lights of the cabin. Traveling through the woods at night was difficult, but he somehow made his way. As he approached the cabin, he noticed that there were no cars parked in front of the house. *Funny*, he thought. The lights were on inside, and the sounds of rock and roll music were coming from the rear of the cabin, penetrating the night air. John peeked in one of the front windows to see if anyone was inside, but no one was. He thought maybe they were out back. So being as quiet as he could, he crept around to the back of the cabin.

There was Nick, enjoying a cigar while sitting on the lake's edge fishing. It was apparent that he was not concerned with anything but simply enjoying a pleasant and peaceful evening. *This is too easy*, John thought to himself. He carefully looked around to see if he could see Telly, but he was nowhere to be found. John decided to move into position, so he quickly and quietly crept up behind Nick. Nick, feeling someone move up behind him, quickly turned and looked up at John who was standing there in the darkness. John said, "Remember me?" in a deep tone. A startled and surprised Nick tried to quickly scramble to his feet. However, John was prepared. He immediately hit Nick over the head with his revolver, knocking him out.

John then took Nick's fishing line and used it to secure his hands and feet with many wrappings around each. He then tied fishing hooks to the line in various locations to provide maximum pain if Nick tried to free himself. After securing the house and the grounds, John realized that Telly wasn't anywhere to be found. Being a big man himself, about six feet three and two-hundred-plus pounds, John grabbed Nick by his hair and dragged him into the cabin. Nick was moaning in pain, and when he became more coherent, John started probing him on the whereabouts of Telly.

"Where's Telly?" he asked.

"Who? Telly. You're looking for Telly. Well, he's not here. I can take you to him. Just cut me loose," Nick replied with a nervous grin.

"I don't think so. Now where's Telly?" John asked as he kicked Nick in the side.

Nick rolled and grimaced with pain as he began thrashing about, trying to get free. However, the fishing hooks did their job as they sank into Nick's flesh. With each thrashing struggle to get free, the hooks sank deeper until he realized it was useless to keep trying.

As Nick gave up his effort to get free, John began to laugh and said in a sarcastic tone, "Do you like that, Nick? Wait till you see what I have planned next!" He then kicked Nick again saying, "Now where is Telly?"

Nick, not seeing the humor, looked up at John. Feeling the pain from the fish hooks and trembling with anger, he said, "You better hope I don't get out of this." John just stood there and laughed sarcastically while looking down at Nick. "I'll tear your eyeballs out!" shouted Nick.

John stopped laughing, squatted down over Nick, and said with a more serious tone in his voice, "But, Nick, you won't. You won't get out of this!"

John then turned away from Nick and walked into the kitchen. Not realizing, he began to whistle a song called "Take Me Home, Country Roads" by

John Denver that he and his wife used to listen to throughout their long relationship. He was looking for something else to use on Nick to get him to talk. As he was looking about the kitchen, Nick was curiously watching John from his location on the floor. He squirmed carefully around to get a better look into the kitchen area. He could hear the drawers to the cabinets opening and then slamming shut, utensils being shuffled about making a clinging noise that seemed to make Nick nervous.

Suddenly, Nick realized where he had heard that toon. A sarcastic, devilish laugh began to echo throughout the cabin. "Hey, I've heard that song before. As a matter of fact, I heard it the night we killed your wife." John stopped whistling and stood frozen. He clinched his gun and removed it from its holster. He wanted to put a bullet through his head, but he realized that that's exactly what Nick wanted him to do. He slowly holstered his gun and began whistling again, not allowing Nick the satisfaction of letting him see his pain. "Did you hear me?" shouted Nick. Hey, I asked if you heard me in there."

John ignored him and continued looking through the kitchen for something that he could use on Nick. All the while, his whistling got louder and more intense. "This is more like it," John said.

Suddenly, John's whistling stopped as he said to Nick, "You know, Nick, I've come to realize that I'm a lot like you in some ways."

"Yeah. How's that?"

"I've come to realize that I enjoy causing excruciating pain to guys like you," John said with his own devilish, sarcastic laugh. "Now isn't that funny, Nick?"

"Yeah, well, you can go to hell!" shouted Nick nervously.

"Now, Nick, really, that's not very nice. Ah, this will work just fine," John said as Nick tried to raise his head to see what John had found.

John walked over to Nick, carrying a pair of pliers. He bent down waving the pliers in the air, making sure that Nick could see them. Nick began to look extremely nervous.

John smiled and said, "Now, Nick, we can do this the easy way or the hard way. It's completely up to you. What is truly amazing, Nick, is that I have recently discovered that I get the most response out of people when their digits are at stake. It's amazing. Watch, I'll show you."

Nick said with a surprised and frantic look on his face, "Huh?" as John quickly grabbed his little finger and placed it into the grips of the pliers. "Now wait. Wait. Wait a minute!" yelled Nick.

Before John could apply any pressure to the pliers, he noticed car headlights flickering through the front window of the cabin. He quickly gagged Nick and dragged him behind the couch and out of sight. John then took a position near the front door and waited for Telly to make his way into the cabin.

The door opened, and Telly entered, saying, "Nick. Nick, I got some news."

Just then, John stuck his revolver to the back of Telly's head, saying, "Hello, Telly. We've been waiting for you. Please sit down."

John then directed Telly toward the chair in front of the TV. Telly sat down. A frantic and confused look came over his face. He began fidgeting, much like that of an adolescent in trouble. "Oн god, they told me you would be coming. It was Nick, not me. I swear." Telly looked around and noticed Nick's feet sticking out from behind the couch. He suddenly leaped up and tried to make a run for the back door, but before he could get very far, John fired a shot into his stomach. He fell back into the chair, screaming in pain. John walked up and squatted down in front of Telly, watching him cringe in pain.

"Gutshot. What a shame. It won't be long now," said John.

Telly said, "Please. I don't want to die!" as he held his stomach and cried with pain.

"How old are you, son?" asked John.

"Twenty-six," he replied.

As Telly was weakening and becoming close to death, John said with a serious tone in his voice, "Telly, can you hear me? You listen and know this as you take your last breath. My son was ten years old and my daughter was only eight. They had their entire lives in front of them, and you and Nick took that away. Now I'm going to take your life away from you."

While Telly sat dying in the chair, not being able to move, John reached around the counter and pulled out a jug of lighter fluid that he had found earlier. He began to spray the curtains, the floor, and the furniture, emptying the jug. He pulled Nick around from behind the couch and left him lying on the floor in the middle of the room. Nick was struggling now more than ever to get loose, but the hooks were too much to overcome.

As John took out the gag from Nick's mouth, he said, "You boys like fire, then you'll love this." John took out a match and lit it as Nick began to scream for his life. John stood there for an instant looking at Nick and Telly, then he dropped the match on the floor. The floor burst into flames and quickly spread across the cabin, igniting everything in its path. "This is for my wife and kids," he said in a sad, soft tone.

Both men were screaming for help, hoping that maybe he would change his mind and take them into custody, but John simply turned and walked outside. As he began to make his way back to his car, he could hear the two men's screams echoing through the darkness.

The wood cabin burned quickly, and it wasn't long before the screams of the two men were no longer heard, and all was quiet.

CHAPTER 6

As John left the area—leaving behind the memories of the burning cabin, which lit up the night sky and the screams of Nick and Telly—he wanted to feel better now that he had succeeded with his revenge, but he didn't. It was as though he had accomplished his primary goal in life. *Now what do I do?* he wondered to himself. He had hoped that by doing all this, it would somehow make him feel better and maybe he could go forward with his life. It seemed that just the opposite had occurred. He was now more alone than ever, and with what he had done, he became the same type of man as Nick and Telly were. His actions of that night were of a cold and heartless insane person who only wanted harm to come to those he hated. John would have to conceal this from society forever, but forever it would be etched deep into his soul. He realized this as he began his long drive home back to his empty apartment.

As he drove, he went into a trancelike daydream. He began thinking of the last day that he had spent with his family. That cool fall Saturday morning, how he could feel the enthusiasm and excitement in the air as the young athletes played their game. He remembered the scenes of that day as they played through his mind like a home movie. His son was taking the pitchout and running around the end for a sixty-five-yard touchdown. He could hear the screams of joy from the stands as his son crossed the goal line for the score. He remembered with the vividness of slow motion as his son turned and looked into the stands, making sure that he was watching. In his mind, he could see his wife and daughter cheering as he made his run and his daughter yelling in an ever-so-proud voice, "That's my big brother!" The vivid memories of that day became too much for John to bear as he began to wipe the tears away from his eyes.

As John's eyes began to clear, he looked at the gas gauge and realized that he was almost out of gas. The idea of having to stop at that log cabin convenience store for gas made him nervous. However, he had to. He had no choice. He hoped that they were still open, but at the same time, he hoped that they were not. As he pulled up to the gas pump, he noticed that the lights inside the store were still on. He turned on the pump and began pumping gas while keeping an eye out for the old man. *I hope that old coot doesn't come out here*, he thought to himself. He just wanted to fill up and be on his way as quickly as possible. As the pump stopped, he knew that he had to go inside and pay, which he was dreading.

He walked to the door and pulled out his money as he wanted to pay and get out of there as fast as possible. He walked inside and immediately noticed a different guy standing behind the counter, a younger man, probably in his forties.

John couldn't help but ask, "Where's pops?"

"Pops. Who? What are you talking about?" the clerk said with a confused look.

"You know, the old man that was here earlier tonight."

"There hasn't been any old man here. Just me," replied the clerk.

John began to smile, saying, "No, there was an old man behind the counter earlier. I bought some stuff and gave him some money for it."

"This money?" the clerk asked as he held up ten dollars.

"Yeah," replied John with a bewildered look.

The clerk said, "I was wondering where this came from. It didn't add up to the register. Thanks!"

"Sure, now what happened to the old man?" asked John for a second time.

The clerk smiled, shook his head, and walked out from behind the counter. He motioned for John to follow him to the back of the store. As they got to the back of the store, John noticed hundreds of photographs on the wall. Apparently, these were pictures of fishermen that had been made throughout the years. They were all showing off their catch. The store clerk pointed to one picture located in the center of the wall with a big red circle around it.

"This old man?" he asked.

John leaned in to get a closer look at the picture. It was him all right.

"Yeah, that's him," replied John.

"I thought that's who you were talking about. That's our ghost," said the store clerk as he began to smile.

"Are you serious—a ghost?"

"Oh yeah, I'm very serious. He died shortly after this picture was taken. He loved it out here. He was a fishing maniac," said the clerk.

John stood there, listening as he took a second look at the picture.

"Well, that looks like him all right."

"Oh yeah, that's him. I've personally never seen him, but some of our regular customers have," the clerk replied.

John, in disbelief, noticed that the picture was dated August 1975, and he looked exactly as he did at the counter earlier that evening. *If he's not a ghost, then the old man hasn't aged a day in twenty-plus years*, he thought.

"Man, you're pulling my leg. The guy in here earlier must have been his son or younger brother or somebody like that. Come on."

The clerk looked over at John while nodding his head and said, "Yep, it's him all right. He seems to appear and offer advice only to the troubled ones. I guess that's why he's never appeared to me," as he smiled.

Not sure what to think about the whole thing, John paid for his gas and left the convenience store, never wanting to return.

He drove away, somewhat troubled and trying to make some sense of the two individuals at the store. He thought to himself, *They're just playing a prank. They probably do this sort of thing all the time. All they had to do was ink in the date on that picture.* John started to laugh as he began to feel better due to his logical explanation. *They really had me going*, he thought to himself.

As he drove, he was becoming very tired, for it had been a long day. The highway was dark, and his eyes were becoming heavy. He was still only halfway home. The radio in his car was off, and all was quiet, very quiet, as he began to relax.

Giving full attention to the road ahead and not thinking of anything else, he suddenly thought he heard an unusual voice coming from the back seat. It was a soft whispering voice, almost as though he had imagined hearing someone say something. *What was that?* he wondered.

He noticed that an unusual chill began to fill the inside of his car, making it suddenly very cold, so he immediately turned up the heater. It was already a frigid night but not this cold. The frost from his breath began to form ice on the inside of the window of his car. "What's going on? Don't tell me my defroster is out," he said out loud as he began to wipe away the ice.

Again, he heard something, like a soft whisper. John turned quickly toward the back seat to see if someone was back there, but there wasn't anyone. "Man, I must be getting tired!" he said to himself.

Listening intently, he waited to hear the strange noise again, but it did not come. He waited and waited and waited, but nothing unusual happened.

Finally, after settling down, he began to refocus his attention on the road. Then, again, he heard a soft-spoken whispering voice, only clearly this time.

The voice said, "Do you believe? John, do you believe?" John turned quickly.

"What? What's that?" he asked with a confused look.

This time, he pulled the car over to the side of the road, quickly got out, and opened the back door. He just knew that someone had to be in the back seat, but there was no one. He opened the trunk and looked in. Still, nothing.

After finding no reason for the noise, he was now wide awake. *I didn't imagine that*, he thought. John stood on the side of the road, looking at his car. Now a little shaken by the voice, he wasn't too anxious to get back in, but he knew he had to. He simply couldn't figure out what that noise could have been. John took his time getting back in the car as he searched the car for a second time and a third.

Finally, he convinced himself that it must have been the wind. Now nervous and more wide awake than ever, he drove onward with the radio playing as loud as he could possibly tolerate.

CHAPTER 7

John made it home without any more unusual events occurring that evening. As he got out of his car, he stood there looking at it and wondered to himself what actually had happened. A bit puzzled and confused, he decided to go inside his apartment. He immediately went over to the refrigerator where he had plenty of beer in stock. He thought to himself, *I need a stiff drink. Yeah, a stiff drink. That's what I need. Maybe then I can relax*. He poured a full beer into a mug and then poured a shot of Crown Royal.

John then dropped the shot into the mug and slammed the whole thing down in four giant gulps. He wiped the dribble off his bearded chin and immediately repeated the procedure. In less than five minutes, he had consumed two beers and two shots of Crown. As he completed his second drink, he said, "Now that's what I'm talking about. I already feel better!"

Since John hadn't eaten much of anything the past couple of weeks, it wasn't long before the drinks began to work their magic on John. He grabbed another beer and made his way to the couch. Being that he was living in a fully furnished rented apartment, one can only imagine how uncomfortable the furnishings were. He found it especially difficult to sleep in his bed at night by himself. After being married for as long as John had been, he found it difficult to sleep alone. He had grown comfortable having his wife next to him at night, and he just couldn't seem to get used to her not being there. Therefore, John was in no hurry to go to bed.

As he made his way to the couch, he picked up the black box that he had retrieved from his house. It seemed that this black box was now the most important possession in his life. John sat on the couch, drinking his beer, and slowly looked through the box. In it were memories of his life with his family.

He removed each item very carefully, not wanting to damage anything in any way. He then laid them out on the coffee table in some sequential order that only he would know. Once John had his items in order, he then began to pick up each one, holding the item and staring at it. Each item had a special memory, reminding him of some special event that he had shared with his family.

Emotionally, John was a wreck, and spiritually, he had questions. He just couldn't understand how these things could have happened to his family. He felt guilty because he knew his actions and his career had caused his family's doom, yet he was angry because he always believed that they would be safe because of his spiritual beliefs. These issues weighed heavily on his mind as he sat on the couch, drinking himself to sleep. As he slept, he slept peacefully and alone on the uncomfortable couch in the dark dingy apartment. Just him with no noise of little ones running about and no laughter to lift his spirits.

John awoke the next morning to the sound of a bird outside his window. It was a strange-looking creature, resembling the markings of a blue jay, but it was white instead of blue with gray makings instead of black. It was pecking and squawking as though he wanted to come inside. So he went over to the window to have a closer look. The bird was sitting on the window ledge looking back at him. *That's a bit odd*, he thought. *What's that bird doing?* he wondered. As the two exchanged glances, John slowly opened the window. The bird just sat there showing no fear. John turned and walked into the kitchen area to retrieve some bread for the bird to eat. He thought, *This bird must be starving. He has no fear. Any other bird would have flown away when I opened that window.*

As John got into the kitchen, he heard the flutter of wings. Looking back at the bird, he noticed that it had flown into the apartment and was sitting on the coffee table. It just sat there looking at John, apparently with no fear or nervousness. John grabbed a piece of bread and began tearing off pieces. He tossed the bread to the bird, and to John's delight, the bird caught every piece.

John smiled and said, "Well, bird, you looking for a place to live? You know, I could use a roommate." John began chewing on a piece of bread himself as he continued to talk to the bird. "I wouldn't expect you to understand, but I've had a pretty rough time of things lately."

John spoke as if he were waiting for a reply from the bird, but none came. Instead, he just sat there focused on John, observing his every movement. The bird then began to walk back and forth on the table as if he were pacing. John thought, *You must really be hungry*. So he got another piece of bread and began tossing more pieces over to the bird.

"Well, I didn't think you would understand my troubles. You're just a bird," John said as he began to smile. He then suddenly thought of something else, saying, "Hey! If you want to stay here, there is only one rule: no pooping in the house. If you have to poop, then let me know." The bird then cocked his head and looked at John as if he were saying that he understood. "That's right. That's right. Just wink or squawk or something. I don't know. I guess we'll figure each other out."

As John finished talking, the bird let out a squawk and then flew out of the window. Feeling a bit sad to see his new friend leave so suddenly, John ran over to the window and yelled for the bird to return, but he didn't.

After his unexpected visit from the blue jay, another strange feeling came over him. He sat down on the couch and thought about what he had done over the past few days.

John had thought that by killing these people to avenge his family, it would in some way make him feel better, but it didn't. He felt worse. He thought about Nick, Telly, and the man at the docks. They were mean, immoral, corrupt people who probably deserved everything they got. And then there was Jimmy. He probably deserved more than any of the other three to get what was coming to him, but John knew he wouldn't be the one to do such evil. He knew that Jimmy had crossed the line when he did what he did to John's family. Even the mob has rules about attacking innocent family members, and John knew that this would not sit well with the mob bosses. "No, I'll let the mob take care of Jimmy," John said to himself.

John suddenly had an overwhelming desire to go to church. He got dressed and went to the nearest church for confessional. Upon entering, he noticed a giant cross in the forefront that greeted all who came through the doors. A feeling of peace and good will came over John. It was a feeling that he longed for, a feeling that made him feel a little like his old self. He looked over at the confessionals and hesitantly approached. Still feeling troubled, he wasn't sure if he was ready for this, so he entered with some reluctance.

John began by saying, "Bless me, Father, for I have sinned." And then he became silent, taking a deep breath.

The priest said, "I'm here, son. Please continue."

"Yes. Yes. I'm sorry. It's been three months and six days since my last—" John paused again and began to weep.

"Son, what troubles you? How can I help?"

"That's just it. You can't. Don't you get it? You can't help!" replied John.

"What is it? Maybe I can help. Just let God in your heart," said the priest.

John let out a sarcastic laugh and said, "Let God in my heart. I've done that. What is all this anyway? This is not real. It's just some big elaborate hoax or something, like Santa Claus and the tooth fairy when we were children. This is not real. There is nothing beyond this, no one to protect us. This is all there is, isn't it?"

"I'm sorry you feel that way, but I assure you that there is a place for us beyond this world. He has a plan for each of us," the priest replied.

"How do you know? We were good people, my family, my wife and kids. We were good people. They didn't deserve what happened to them. What kind of a plan was that? What kind of a plan would destroy my family?"

"Son, throughout our lives, we have challenges, trials, and tests that God puts before us. We don't always understand why he does what he does, but we must put our lives in his hands, no matter what, so he can show us the way—his way."

"The way. The way. The way to where? Where was God when my family was being murdered? I don't understand. My daughter, my beautiful eight-year-old daughter, my ten-year-old son, and my innocent wife who only wanted to love her family. Where was God when they needed him most?" replied an angry John.

The Father grew quiet upon hearing this from John. He seemed to struggle for the right words to say. Just as he began to try to convince John that he should enter into their family-crisis classes, he heard the door to the confessional open and then shut. As John left, the Father felt terrible that he was unable to say the right words to help him. He only hoped that John would return someday and that he might have a second chance to help.

John left the church and wandered around the street, not knowing exactly where he was heading. His attempt at the church seemed to make things worse, not better, and he was now more lost in this world than ever. Soon, he wandered by a liquor store. He went inside and purchased two cases of beer, one gallon of Crown Royal, and one loaf of bread for the bird, hoping he would return.

As John got home, he immediately began his drinking sequence from the previous night. He sat on the couch looking through his black box, drinking and hoping that his bird friend would return, but the bird didn't. As the evening passed by and the alcohol took effect, he soon fell asleep as he had the previous night.

For the next two years, John lived a lonely meager life. Full of self-pity and doubt, he would go out only for food and refresh his supply of liquor. He kept up with the world around him by reading the paper and didn't seem too interested in television. He would read a book or two to escape his seclusion.

He found a bar nearby, which was located around the corner from his apartment. It was named O'Mally's. Patrick, the bartender, soon knew John as one of his Friday and Saturday night regulars. Keeping to himself, it was rare that anyone approached John at the bar for conversation. Usually, it would be someone asking John for some beer money, which he would oblige without saying a word. They would simply say, "Thank you," and go on their way, leaving him to himself.

After a few years, the drinking and lack of a proper diet began to take their toll. He barely resembled the man that he once was. He had lost weight and was supporting a healthy beard. Simply, John preferred to fade away from society and all those that were once his friends. To them, he had just disappeared.

CHAPTER 8

John hadn't changed much in the way that he carried out his daily activities. However, the beginning of an uncertain future was beginning to unfold. It all started on a Thursday afternoon. He was on his way to the grocery store when a large black car pulled up alongside the curb. It seemed to be out of place.

As John got closer to the vehicle, he began to slow down, taking notice of the unusually dark-tinted windows. Just as John began to walk past, two men jumped out of the car, grabbed him, and threw him in the back seat.

"Hey, what's going on?" John shouted.

"Are you Mr. O'Roark?" asked one of the men. John was reluctant to answer as the man asked a second time with a more serious tone. "Are you John O'Roark?" he asked again.

John answered, "Yes," with a nervous and cautious feeling.

After receiving the answer that they desired, the car raced off with John inside, wondering to himself what was going on. His heart was pounding as he began to take in his situation. He thought to himself, *I guess this is it. Jimmy finally caught up with me.* The men in the car didn't appear to be too friendly. They didn't say a word to John as they traveled at a high rate of speed. They had a dark and intense look on their faces, not the kind of guys you would want to tell a bad joke to. John had time to look at each one carefully, but he didn't recognize any of them.

John asked, "Where are we going?" None of the men replied or even looked his way. They kept their eyes on the road in front of them, apparently headed to a specific location. John thought that these men must be carrying out specific orders from Jimmy.

As they traveled along, John began to assess the situation, trying to figure a way out of this. John thought to himself, *Maybe I can catch one of these guys off guard. If the car slows down enough, I can jump out.* But it never did. Once they got on the freeway, they just went faster, and John was not in the physical shape that he used to be in. He quickly realized that he would have to ride this out while waiting for another chance.

As they began to leave the city, one of the men turned to John and said, "Now we are going to pull over. Just relax and don't try anything," as if he was reading John's mind. John began to look around to get his bearings as the car quickly pulled to a stop.

One of the men grabbed John and said, "Mr. O'Roark, I'm sorry but I have to put this blindfold on you." His tone surprised John. *Mr. O'Roark*, he thought. *That's strange.*

John reluctantly nodded and said, "Okay."

With the blindfold secure, the car sped off again. John was unsure of exactly what was happening. Usually, guys who want to knock you off are not polite enough to address you as Mr. Anybody.

They drove for about thirty minutes, somewhere south of the metropolitan area. Finally, it felt as though they turned off the main road. From the change of the feel of the road, it seemed they were now on a dirt road. After a few more minutes, the car came to stop. John's mind began to race, thinking the worst, and his heart was pounding in his chest. He thought to himself, *Well, this is it. Good or bad, I'll know soon what this is all about.*

As they took the blindfold off, John's eyes started adjusting to the light. He began to look around at his surroundings. He noticed that they were in a huge farm field. And the only thing for miles was this barn where they had parked. Suddenly, two giant doors slid open as three more men stepped out of the barn. John thought, *Jimmy's boys all right. I'm definitely done.*

Upon realizing that he was doomed, a surge of energy ran through his body. Without hesitation, he headbutted the man standing next to him as they got out of the car. The only thing he knew to do was to start running before they started shooting. The man he headbutted slumped to his knees as John bolted. A second man standing behind John that he had failed to see quickly pulled his pistol and hit John over the head. John blacked out and fell to the ground.

As he slowly began to come to, he found himself inside the barn sitting in a chair with one of the men softly patting him on his face. He could hear someone saying, "Are you okay? Wake up. Wake up." Just then, someone threw water in his face, which felt like a thousand needles. John jumped in his chair as the water hit, and he could hear someone saying to one of the other men, "Ray, you better be glad he's coming around or it will be your ass." John managed to look over at the man who was getting it from the other guy as he seemed to look quite anxious for John to come to.

One of the men, noticing that John was coming to, walked over to him and said sincerely, "I'm sorry, Mr. O'Roark. I didn't mean to hit you that hard."

"What's going on?" John yelled as his head began to throb.

Just then, another man stood up from a chair located against the wall where he had been sitting. He had been leaning back in his chair, waiting for John to come to. Everyone else was standing around as the attention focused on the man that just stood up. He was smoking a cigar, and as he approached John, he exuded an air of confidence equal to no other. He walked slowly up to John and knelt down in front of him. He was less than a foot away, looking deeply into John's eyes. He just stayed there staring into John's eyes as John became more nervous than ever. John gathered his inner strength and stared back at the man. He didn't want to give the impression to this guy that he was being intimidated by him. After what seemed to be an extended amount of time, John felt confident that he had succeeded as the man began to smile.

He leaned in closer to John and asked in a soft, confident tone, "Do you know who I am?" John looked straight back into the man's eyes, trying to project his own confidence.

He said with a strong voice, "I haven't a clue who you are!"

"Good," the man said while nodding his head up and down.

He then stood up, turned, and started walking away from John toward the darkened area in the back of the barn. As he walked away from John, he raised his hand and with a waving motion, signaled to someone in the dark area of the barn. Almost immediately, the lights turned on in that area. John could see that they had someone tied up and gagged in a chair. *I hope that's not Dex*, he thought to himself. Whoever it was was totally restrained without the ability to move or speak. The headman or boss in the center of the area made another waving motion toward John's direction. Two men immediately came over to John and said, "Come over here with us, Mr. O'Roark." No one seemed to move or speak without the direction of the boss.

They led John into the small area in the back of the barn where he was able to get a closer look at the guy who was tied up. As John got closer, he realized who this guy was. It was Jimmy. He had been beaten severely. "Jimmy," John said with a soft and surprised voice. John could feel everyone's eyes on him as if they were waiting to see how he would react. Standing less than five feet away from Jimmy, John had an overwhelming urge to take someone's gun and blow Jimmy's head off. He had waited so long for this opportunity.

As he felt the rage roaring through his body, John began to think of his family and what Jimmy had done to them. He stood there staring at Jimmy in a trancelike state as the memories of his family raced through his mind. Everyone could see the anger in John's face as the boss leaned into John and said in a soft whispering yet powerful tone, "Jimmy committed a terrible offense against your family. For that, we regret. It's not our style to do what he did. Family is sacred." He reached out and patted John's shoulder.

As the boss became angrier, he said in a louder and more hostile tone, "You never attack another man's family! That was his mistake. He knew better, and now he must pay for that mistake."

John's anger peaked as he stood listening to the boss. Suddenly, his trancelike state broke due to an odd noise that he heard coming from the rafters. He hoped that after they finished with Jimmy, he wouldn't be next.

"We don't blame you for taking the action that you did against Nick and Telly. They were hotheads anyway. But the other guy at the docks, that was brutal!" he said as everyone began to laugh.

Just then, John heard the strange noise again coming from the rafters. He looked up and saw what looked like one of those birds staring down from a beam. He seemed to be observing everything that was going on. When John saw that bird, a settling feeling came over him as he remembered his bird friend from the apartment. How John waited and wished for two years that that silly bird would return. And then he thought to himself, *What a time to be thinking of a bird.*

The boss signaled for someone to give him a gun. Immediately, the biggest guy in the barn stepped up to the boss, handing him his pistol. John couldn't help realizing that that was the guy he had headbutted earlier because he was wearing a hefty red spot on his forehead. *Great*, John thought to himself. *If I do get out of here, this guy is probably going to beat me into next week.*

The boss took the gun and then held it out for John to take, saying, "Here. Now finish it," as he pointed toward Jimmy. John looked down at the gun and stared at it. His hands trembled as he stood there, thinking about taking the gun. He started clinching his fists as he almost accepted the gun, but he couldn't. John looked over at Jimmy. He was sitting there tied up while squirming and trying to free himself. Everyone's eyes were on John as though they were coaxing him to take the gun.

After what seemed to be several minutes of silence and intense pressure, John said, "I can't."

"Here. Take it. Finish it," replied the boss.

John replied by saying, "Will it bring my wife and kids back? No, it won't! Will it? This is your thing, your rule, your code of ethics. You do it."

The boss stood there looking at John in aggravation as he dropped the gun down to his side and began bouncing it off his leg. He just stood there looking at John. He started nodding his head and getting more upset while looking intensely into John's eyes. Finally, he said, "All right then!"

He immediately turned and quickly fired one shot at Jimmy, hitting him in the center of the chest. Jimmy let out a moan and slumped down in the chair. As his body relaxed, the boss tossed the gun back to the man who had given it to him.

He then pulled out a handkerchief and started wiping off his hands while continuing to look at John straight in his eyes. John, not wanting to show any fear at this point, looked straight back at the boss. John noticed his cold black eyes. This man was very high in the organization, and he demanded respect from everyone. His cold, hard look alone sent a deep penetrating fear that he felt in his bones. He then eased closer to John within inches of his face. John could smell the cigar on his breath as he began to talk. He said in a soft confident tone, "This finishes it. No more vengeful acts between our families."

John took a long pause, staring straight back into the boss's eyes. Neither man said a word. No one in the building moved or spoke as everyone eagerly anticipated John's response. The anxiety of the moment made seconds seem like long lingering minutes.

John began seeing flashing images in his mind of his wife and children and the horrors that they must have endured when they were murdered.

Then suddenly, the intense moment was broken by a simple squint of the eyes from the mob boss, which caught John's attention.

"Well," he asked.

With a firm tone in his voice, John responded, "Fine with me. It's finished."

The boss turned to his men and said, "Take him back."

Everyone in the barn began moving about as John started to feel relieved. He was taken to the car, blindfolded, and driven home. There was no conversation, and John hoped that the men obeyed their boss. He just knew that the big guy was going to do a number on him as payback for the earlier headbutt. However, he made it home without any further incident with the men. It seemed to be over as suddenly as it had begun.

Feeling fortunate to still be alive, John went home as quickly as he could, forgetting about the grocery store. Upon entering the apartment, he secured the doors immediately. He then went to the refrigerator and began making one of his beer and Crown Royal drinks. Only this time, he used a double shot of Crown. Suddenly, he heard an unusual noise, a loud squawk. Still a bit edgy, John dove behind the refrigerator door while his drink went flying.

"Who's that?" he yelled as his heart began to race. He heard no response other than another squawking noise. *What in the world,* he said to himself.

As he began to relax, he was able to make his way into the living room area. Now that he had caught his breath and was in control of his senses, he thought that sounded like that bird. He noticed a movement on the coffee table, and to his delight, it was his bird friend, the blue jay.

"Well, I thought you had flown South or something," John said with a smile. The bird squawked as if to say he was glad to be back. "You know, you're the second blue jay I've seen today," said John.

Just then, he heard another noise that sounded like the fluttering of wings. He looked over at the window and saw two more birds on the ledge. They suddenly took flight and flew into the apartment. Landing on the coffee table alongside the other bird, the three began to take turns squawking. *This is very strange*, John thought to himself. "It looks like you brought some friends with you this time," he said as he smiled.

John went to the kitchen and got some bread. He had always kept fresh bread around in hopes that the bird would return. He began tearing off small pieces from bread and tossed them to the birds. To his delight, they seemed to take turns making fantastic acrobatic catches. John spent the rest of the evening playing with the birds as they seemed to be enjoying it as much as John. He was delighted, and it turned out to be the best evening he had spent in years.

"It's been two years. Where have you been?" asked John. Giving no reply, the birds just sat there looking at him, bobbing their heads back and forth. "Well, you're welcome here anytime, anytime you want. After the day I had, you're a welcome sight." John lay back against the softness of the couch as his exhausted body began to relax. He closed his eyes and then began mumbling over and over to himself, "What do I do now? What do I do? What do I do?" until he fell into a deep sleep.

CHAPTER 9

It was Friday morning, and John was waking to the sounds of squawking blue jays. As he woke, he wondered to himself if he had been dreaming as he was remembering the events of yesterday. Hearing the birds squawking and fluttering about, he quickly realized that he had not been dreaming. He realized that his troubles with Jimmy and the mob were over and that gave him a renewed sense of freedom. However, he knew that things would never be the same.

Remembering those last few words that the mob boss had said touched a deep nerve inside John. His saying, "No more vengeance between our families," in some way didn't seem fair. John's family was gone, all of them. They were not coming back nor could they be replaced. John thought, *What am I supposed to do? Go on as though nothing has ever happened? Is my family these three blue jays now?* Somehow thinking of this made John angry, angry to the point that he began taking it out on the birds.

For a while, the birds gave John a sense of pleasure. As long as they were around, he had something to occupy his time, allowing him to escape from his inner pain. But now, just the opposite was occurring. He was beginning to see the blue jays as a reminder of his family. To him, the idea of replacing his family with these birds was tormenting. He felt that it was as though Jimmy and the mob were getting one last shot at him.

John's rage began to peak, and his hands started to tremble. Soon, he began chasing the birds out of his apartment. The birds, realizing that they were no longer welcome, started to get excited. They flew about the room in a panic as John began to swat at them with a flyswatter.

Finally, two of the three birds flew out of the window, landing on the ledge just outside. The third bird, which was his original friend, the first bird ever to appear to John, made his way to the window ledge as well. He sat there looking back at John. John stopped chasing the birds and stood there looking at them. It was as though they were all saying goodbye.

At that instant, John realized that he had made a terrible mistake, but it was too late. The birds, with their one last look, let out a squawk and flew away. John suddenly felt a new kind of trembling feeling surge throughout his entire body. Looking down, he noticed that his right hand was shaking. He grabbed his right hand with his left and held on for a minute to stop the shaking, but it didn't help.

As soon as he let go, his hand began to shake again. He realized that he hadn't had a drink in more than twenty-four hours. When he came in yesterday and noticed the birds, he got distracted and forgot to finish making his drink.

"Those dang birds," he said to himself as he smiled. *I was so caught up in playing with those birds. I forgot all about my drink*, he thought as he began scratching his head. His hands continued to shake, and it hit John just then that it wasn't his anger causing his shaking. He suddenly realized that he had a drinking problem and that the alcohol was causing his shaking. John thought, *I can control this. I just won't drink anymore. It's not as though I have to have a drink.*

He then decided to go to the store since he never got to finish his shopping from yesterday. After changing his list and leaving off all alcoholic beverages, he headed out. It wasn't long before the trembling in his hands got worse. It seemed the closer he got to the store, the worse it got. He stood there at the front entrance of the store looking down at his hands. *This is terrible*, he thought. "I can't go in there. I would be too embarrassed for anyone to see this," he said, speaking softly to himself. He decided that if he had one drink, it would settle his shaking enough that he could complete his shopping. *I'll go to Omally's and have one drink. That's it. Just one. That'll get me by. That's all I need*, he thought. Instead of one beer, he had two. And it wasn't long before he was slamming down his favorite mix, The Boiler Maker.

John stopped counting the number of drinks that he had. He even began convincing himself as to why it was okay to have one more. The problem was that there was always just one more, and it became easier and easier to justify having that next drink. Soon, it didn't matter anymore.

It was about eleven o'clock at night, and John didn't realize that he had been there for as long as he had. He felt guilty that he let himself down, and he wasn't strong enough to keep from drinking for just this one day. He promised himself that tomorrow he would stop. "This is it. This is definitely the last drink for a while. I won't have a drink for a week, one week. I can do that. After all, it's not as though I have to have a drink," he said as he finished his last beer. Somehow he knew he was making himself an empty promise.

He sat at the table and looked around the bar, noticing that these were the same people who were always there. *For years, it's the same people every Friday and Saturday night,* he thought to himself. *I always thought that they were just a bunch of out-of-work drunks.* John turned as he began to get up from his chair. He never noticed that behind where he sat was a huge wall mirror.

As he stood up and looked in the mirror, he could see the entire bar in its reflection. With the crowd in the background, he could see himself standing front and center. To his dismay, he realized that he looked just like everyone else.

John, with a new sense of sadness, slowly made his way to the exit. It was a long, narrow bar, and his occasional bumping into his fellow regular bar mates didn't seem to bother anyone. He had become one of them.

As he stepped outside, he looked around. It was late, dark, and John could sense a change in the weather. A thick fog had drifted in as it seemed to be settling on the streets, making for an eerie cool evening. He could feel the heavy dew and mist hitting him on his face. *Strange that there isn't any traffic on the street. It is a quiet, out-of-the-way place, but there is usually some traffic*, he thought to himself.

John, looking ahead, noticed the streetlight on the corner. The light from the lamp gave off a soft glow that seemed to cut through the fog and provided the only light on the dark street. He could feel that the dampness from the night air was getting heavier and heavier as he began his walk toward home.

He hadn't gone very far when he thought he heard an unusual noise. It sounded like someone was talking to him from far away. Being as dark as it was, John stopped to listen.

He heard a faint, whispering type of voice, saying, "John. John, do you believe?"

"What? What did you say? Is someone out there?" he yelled.

The voice was so faint that John wasn't sure he was really hearing it. *Maybe it's just the breeze,* he wondered to himself. Suddenly, he heard the sounds of wings fluttering from above. *I wonder. That sounds like those blue jays,* he thought. After listening for a second, the noises went away. *Probably not,* he thought as he continued on his way.

He looked ahead at the corner where he noticed someone standing under the streetlight. It seemed to be a tall, slender woman. And the way the light fell around her in the fog, it seemed as though she was giving off some sort of glow. John stopped to get a more focused look. He thought, *I don't know who she is, but she's beautiful.* She seemed to be just standing there as if she were waiting for someone. She was tall with long, wavy blond hair. As he approached, she didn't show any signs of fear at all. John came nearer, and they made eye contact for the first time. She seemed to give off an aura of tranquility and peacefulness that caused John to be drawn to her in some way.

Being concerned that this young woman was out very late and not in the safest part of town, he asked, "Are you lost? Can I help?" Her eyes were penetrating, and as she smiled, John had a soothing, sobering feeling shoot through his body.

She looked at John deeply and said with a soft, delicate voice, "No. I'm not lost. I'm actually waiting for you."

"For me?" he replied.

"Yes, for you. You're John O'Roark, aren't you?" she asked.

John, looking a bit surprised, said, "Yes, I am. But how do you know me?"

"A friend," she said. "He told me I could find you here."

John said, "Well, I don't have any friends. My friends are all gone. What friend anyway?"

John took a step back to get a clearer look at the woman. *Maybe I know her from somewhere*, he thought. He realized that he had never seen her before in his life, but she was remarkably beautiful. She seemed to give off a glow as she stood under the light in the fog. *Must be her light-colored dress, this fog, and this lighting that gives her a majestic look*, John thought to himself as he was becoming more entranced with the woman. She realized that John was trying to figure out where they might know each other by his quiet stare.

She said, "John, it doesn't matter who told me you would be here. Why am I here? Well, I need your help."

"Help. Help with what?" asked John.

She leaned forward to get closer to John and said in a soft, innocent, and sweet tone, "A friend of mine when I was younger, well, she was murdered. The people responsible for this have never been brought to justice or even questioned."

Just as she finished, John felt a cold chill of wind blow by, causing him to shiver. He pulled his jacket to him and said, "No. No, I'm sorry, but I don't do that kind of work. Besides, I'm retired."

"I understood that you could help me," she said.

"No, I'm sorry, but I can't," he replied.

"Would you please hear me out before you decide?" she pleaded.

"No. Like I said, I'm retired. You need to find someone else to help you."

As John started to leave the enchanting woman standing under the light, he turned to take one more look. *Something about this woman I can't put my finger on*, he thought. He had barely taken two steps when he stopped and suddenly had this overwhelming feeling of guilt and sadness.

While looking back he said, "Okay, tell me more."

She smiled and said, "Good. I knew you would help me, but can we go somewhere and get out of this weather?"

He nodded and said, "Yeah, sure. I live around the corner from here. We can go there if you don't mind."

"That's fine," she replied with a smile.

"By the way, do you drink coffee?" he asked.

She raised her brow, saying, "I love coffee," as they went on their way.

As they made their way around the corner, John realized that he didn't have any coffee. In fact, he hadn't drunk coffee on a regular basis in some time.

Luckily for John, they were approaching the grocery store where he did most of his shopping. As they got to the front door, John stopped.

"What is it?" she asked.

"I need to go in here and get a few things. I hope you don't mind," he said, feeling a little embarrassed.

"No, I don't mind," she replied.

As the two walked into the store, John looked over at her. *She is more beautiful than I even imagined*, he thought. She was a stunning beauty. As she gracefully moved about the store, John noticed that she was attracting most of the people who were in the store at that late hour. Even the women in the store couldn't help but stare as they, too, noticed her remarkable beauty. John went over to the coffee and picked up a can. As he leaned over, he looked up at her and smiled.

She realized that he was embarrassed for having to buy coffee for the two of them, so she smiled and said playfully, "You mean you invite me to your place for coffee at this late hour, and you don't even have any coffee?"

John began to show an uncomfortable smile while saying with a chuckle, "Yeah. Well, I like mine fresh." Realizing that they had been overheard by a few nearby people, John didn't want anyone to get the wrong impression. He said in a loud tone for those to hear, "No. It's not that. It's not what you think."

She seemed to have a sense of humor because she easily recognized that John was nervous and started to laugh at his embarrassment. Just then, a little sweet, fragile old lady walked by. She looked frail, and she seemed to be about ninety years old.

She looked at John and with a wink, said, "Sure, Willy. Sure," as everyone in the general area began to laugh.

John, with a red face, said, "Okay. Okay, that's funny. That's really funny, Grandma!"

John, still embarrassed, looked over at his newfound friend. She was smiling back as she saw

WILLIAM L HARBEN

the whole event as funny. Then everyone started to laugh, including John.

It suddenly occurred to him that it had been a while since he had last laughed. And with that thought, he abruptly stopped and so did everyone else. "Okay then. Let's pay for this stuff and get out of here."

Suddenly realizing that he didn't even know her name, John stopped before they got to the checkout counter and said, "By the way. I'm sorry. I never got your name."

She smiled and stuck out her hand to shake, saying, "Angelica. My name is Angelica."

As they left the store, he felt good about the idea of having such a beautiful creature by his side. It gave him a feeling of confidence. *She reminds me of my wife in some ways*, he thought to himself. As they completed their walk to his apartment, John suddenly realized that he wasn't drunk anymore, not in the least. *That's strange*, he thought. "I know I drank for several hours today. When I left the bar, I remember that I was stumbling, but I feel great!" he said as he mumbled to himself.

"What's wrong?" she asked.

"Oh, nothing," he said as he opened the door to his apartment.

As they entered his apartment, he thought, *What a mess. Have I been living in this?* He hurriedly began picking up things and putting them in their place. She seemed to overlook his scrambling about, and she made her way into the kitchen where she sat down at the table and waited for John to finish. After determining that it would take a while for him to complete his task, she politely said, "John, don't worry about it. It's just fine."

He stopped as he looked around in disgust at the way he had been living. He then looked over at her where she was patiently waiting. John apologized and said, "Well, I'm sorry. I've had my own problems."

"I know. We all do, but it's what a person does when confronted with those problems. That's what's important," she said as she looked at John and smiled.

John, looking shocked, said, "You know, I've heard that before. An old man told me that, almost those exact words. Now that's strange."

As he thought about what she had said, he began to have a curious feeling. He shook it off and began to brew the coffee. The aroma of fresh brewing coffee seemed to fill the apartment. John closed his eyes and took a deep breath. A flood of memories started racing through his mind, memories of better, more enjoyable times. It reminded him of his old partner, Dex. *I wonder how he's doing*, he thought. It reminded him of the long nights that seemed like an eternity, waiting at the hospital for his children to be born. It reminded him of the late nights that he and his wife stayed up with their son. It seemed that his son would sleep all day, and then when everyone else was ready to go to sleep, he was wide awake and ready to play. He remembered how he and his wife used to joke with each other and how John was going to get revenge on his son for keeping him up all those late nights. John had made a promise to his wife that when his son got old enough, he would have him pruning, edging, weed eating, and mowing the whole neighborhood. It seemed to be an ongoing joke for years between his wife and him, but unfortunately, John never got the chance. All these memories came flowing back to John as he smelled the fresh coffee. *Strange*, he thought. *How so many emotions could be wrapped up in something so simple, like the smell of fresh brewing coffee.*

As he opened his eyes, he turned to look at Angelica. She was sitting at the table and offered a simple smile as John sat down. He said, "Okay, now tell me more about your friend."

CHAPTER 10

It was late as the two sat down at the table. They had their coffee, and she began to tell her story. She took a sip and a deep breath.

Looking into John's eyes, she asked, "Are you ready?"

John said, "Yes. Go ahead, but first, when did this happen exactly?" he asked.

"In 1988," she replied.

"That's a long time ago. We may have a tough time digging up any new info on this thing," he said.

Angelica said, "Yes, you're right, but it's important to me to do what I can. I owe that to Susan."

"Susan," John responded. "Is that the girl's name? I mean your friend?" he asked.

She said, "Yes, Susan Ashworth."

"Wait a minute!" John said as he stood up and began looking for a pen and notepad. "I need something to take some notes," he said.

She looked at him and smiled, waiting patiently for him to return to the table. Not having any success finding what he needed, a frustrated John began mumbling, "Now where are my paper and pens?" just loud enough for her to hear.

"Have you tried this drawer?" she asked as she pointed to a drawer in the kitchen by the stove.

"I don't remember putting them in there," he said with a puzzled look. She just smiled as he went over to the drawer and pulled it open. To his surprise, they were there. "Well, I don't remember putting them in there," he said as he began shaking his head. "Say, are you psychic or something?" he jokingly asked with a chuckle.

"Something like that," she replied with a smile.

John, looking somewhat bewildered, sat down at the table and said, "Okay. Miss Psychic, I'm ready."

He sat down at the table, looking intensely at Angelica, as she began, "Just so you know, you might say I'm a friend of the family. That's why I know so much about what happened to her."

Looking confused, John said, "Wait a minute. I thought you were her good friend."

Hesitantly, she said, "I am, but I'm also a good friend of the family. I just wanted to clear that up so you weren't confused." She said nervously.

"Oh," John replied. "Well, I think I am confused but that's okay. Go ahead," he said with a puzzled look.

She said, "I guess I need to go back to 1986. That's when they met."

"They." Asked John, "Who is they?"

"They would be Kenneth Daultry and his family. Kenneth or Ken, as most of his friends called him, was a law student at Harvard. When they met in 1986, Susan was a young art student attending an art school across town. She was about twenty-one years old and a fabulous young artist with a promising career. She already had had several successful exhibits and had become the talk of the town. At such a young age, her talents were beyond her peers. She was beginning to receive national recognition and was being offered numerous job opportunities from major advertising companies. Susan had a tremendous painting talent, but her true love was sculpture. She was a perfectionist, so she stayed in school to master her sculpturing skills."

John stared at Angelica as she talked. He followed her story intently, only looking down on occasion to take a few notes. As she continued, he could see the anger building in her face as she spoke about Ken.

"Kenneth Daultry was still in school as Susan's fame grew. He was about two years away from graduation and still needed to pass the all-important bar exam. His father, who had a thriving law practice in Colorado, had big plans for Ken when he graduated. Using his influence, Ken's father was planning a major political career for his son. And he was not willing to let anything or anyone stand in the way of his son's success.

"Susan met Ken at one of her exhibitions in the summer of '86. They seemed to be infatuated with each other immediately, and it wasn't long before the two became an item. She was introduced into his circle of friends where she was quickly accepted. It seems that she soon became his trophy because of her reputation as an upcoming artist.

"He seemed to enjoy taking her out to public places where he could show her off. I guess he was trying to make points or build his own reputation among his peers. I'm not sure he ever really loved her or not, but I know she loved him with all her heart."

Angelica, becoming more emotional, asked John if they could take a break. John agreed as he asked, "Do you need a tissue?"

"Yes, please," she said as the tears began to well up in her eyes.

"Are you all right? Would you like some more coffee or something else?" asked John.

As she sniffled, she replied, "No, coffee will be fine."

John made two more cups of coffee as Angelica regained her composure. He turned to her and asked, "This is personally and extremely upsetting for you, isn't it?"

Taking John off guard and with a sudden burst of anger, Angelica said with an intensity that he had not yet witnessed from this gentle beauty, "You have no idea!" as John noticed a revengeful hatred in her eyes.

John was stunned by her response. *Clearly, this woman is somehow involved with this guy named Ken, but I'm not sure how*, he thought. He said, "Okay. Angelica, calm down and tell me more about what happened to Susan."

Angelica nodded and leaned forward, putting her elbows on the table as she continued her story, "About two years had passed after they first met. He had enjoyed taking her to public places and social parties. He would even take her along with his circle of friends to Colorado. Just outside Denver, there was a small lake resort where Ken and his family would vacation every summer. He and his family were well-known and very influential in Colorado but especially in Denver.

"In the spring of '88, Susan began to question their relationship. Graduation was around the corner, and soon after, he would take the bar exam, so she wondered what their future would hold. He was spending a lot of time studying and preparing for his exams and spending less and less time with her. With each passing day, she was becoming more and more insecure about their future. She was afraid that he would pass his tests and then leave her while he pursued his father's wishes. However, she wanted to know if they had a future together. Unfortunately for her, she was unsuccessful in getting the answer that she was wanting. It's not that she got the wrong answer. She didn't get any answer. It was as though she was being pushed aside, which is what she feared.

"Finally, his law student buddies and he took and successfully passed the bar. Susan, thinking that there would be a big night of celebration, was disappointed to find out that her evening with Ken was suddenly canceled.

"Susan didn't understand why and wanted some answers, but Kenneth wasn't making it easy to be found that day. In her search for him, she ended up going to the Harvard law building on campus where he could normally be found. That's when she discovered a flyer on the bulletin board. To her dismay, it read, 'CONGRATULATIONS to all those who PASSED the BAR. LET'S CELEBRATE. PARTY @ RANDY'S HOUSE. [Female law students only. All MALES who passed.]' Girls, let's give 'em a night to remember before we send them on their way." Angelica started to tear up again as she described that flyer. It was amazing that she could remember it so clearly. "Can we take another break?" she asked.

"Yeah, sure. It seems to me that you have a lot of details about their relationship," John said.

"Yeah, so," Angelica said as she wiped away her tears.

John replied nervously, "Well, it's just a bit funny that you have all these details. For example, that note. It's almost like you know that note word for word. Don't you think that's a bit odd?"

"There's nothing odd about it. I told you I was a very good friend of the family. Susan actually kept that note. They found it in her apartment. I've seen it," said Angelica.

"Oh," John said as he nodded. "Would you like another cup of coffee?" he asked.

"Please. That would be good," she said.

They both got up from the table to stretch their legs a bit. John poured another cup of coffee as

Angelica moved into the living room. John was still in the kitchen when he heard the window suddenly shut from the other room. It startled him, for he had always kept it open in case the blue jays ever came back.

"Hey, what are you doing?" he asked.

Angelica, standing in front of the window, looked over at John and said, "You don't need this open anymore," as she smiled.

John said, "Huh, yeah, I guess," looking a little puzzled. He then looked at his watch, saying, "It's a little late. You want to finish this tomorrow?" He asked.

"No, I'm fine if you are. I would like to finish this," replied Angelica.

John said, "Okay," as they both made their way back to the kitchen.

They sat down at the table, and Angelica continued her story, "According to what I heard, it turned out to be a wild party. It was just as the flyer had advertised. Freshman coed law students and all the male law students who had passed their bar exam were there. Susan should have given Ken his night to celebrate, but she didn't. Instead, she kept the flyer and made her way to the party. It was about eleven that night when she arrived. It was in full swing as she walked in the place without so much as a knock. Everyone who knew her was also aware of her two-year relationship with Ken and was shocked to see that she was there. To her dismay, everyone that she knew was avoiding her and not offering any help in locating Ken.

"As she drifted from room to room in her search while practically being ignored, she almost decided to go home and wait until later to confront Ken. But then she noticed Ron who was sitting on the couch next to a young coed. Ron was Ken's closest friend, and she knew that he would know where to find Ken. Susan didn't recognize the girl that Ron was sitting with, and she knew that Julia, his fiancée, wouldn't be too happy with this situation at all. She walked over to Ron and waited for him to look up. It didn't take long, and when he realized that it was Susan, he became very nervous as though he were hiding something. She asked him where she could find Ken.

"His reply was 'Ken. I haven't seen him all night. I thought he was with you.'

"'Hardly,' she replied.

"No more did he finish his lie than the young coed sitting with Ron pointed at a door to her left and started to laugh. Susan could tell that Ron was not happy with the young girl as she made her way through the door.

"The door led her to the backyard. She could hear what seemed to be the jets of a hot tub. As she made her way toward the sounds of the tub, she began hearing laughter. It was Ken and another young coed. Stunned at what she was observing, her heart sank. She simply stood there too devastated to speak. The two were having a night to remember as they were unaware of Susan's presence. Finally, the young girl noticed that they were being watched as she said, 'Ken. Ken. Stop. Someone is watching us.' That's when Ken turned to see Susan standing there, not saying a word. He was shocked and ashamed of his behavior and immediately began trying to explain. But Susan would have nothing to do with his lies. She said, 'There's nothing to explain, and you have nothing I care to hear,' as she turned and walked away. Everyone could hear Ken pleading for Susan to come back so they could talk, but she left without a glance and nothing more to say.

"He tried to call her on the phone for a couple of weeks after that night, but she wouldn't respond. He soon realized that he cared for her more than he thought and was becoming depressed to the point that he was desperate to get her back. The last night that anyone can remember seeing her was when she went out with some friends to a dance club. It was on a Friday evening, and she was with her closest friends. They had decided to go out to help cheer her up. They went to Confetti's, a dance club, and it seemed to be just what she needed. Susan was dancing, drinking, and having the time of her life until she noticed Ken. He was standing there on the edge of the dance floor, just staring at her as she danced. She noticed that he had this eerie look on his face and was making her extremely uncomfortable. It was obvious that he was drunk, but for the time being, he was keeping his distance. She told her friends that he seems obsessed with her. She said that he wouldn't stop following her around. Everywhere she goes, he seems to show up, and he calls constantly, leaving messages for her to call. She said that she was becoming afraid that he may do something desperate. She also told a friend later that night that she didn't want anything more to do with him and that their relationship was over.

"At some point that evening, she had to go to the bathroom.

"She was alone waiting in the hallway where the bathroom was located when he approached her and said, 'Susan, we need to talk!' She was frightened by his sudden appearance and jumped away from him.

"She stared at him and finally said with an angry tone, 'Oh, why don't you just leave me alone?'

"Kenneth was stunned by her remark, and this blank stare came over his face. He had never heard such cruel words from her before, and it seemed to penetrate deep into his heart. That was the last night anyone ever saw her."

Angelica took a deep breath as she finished her story and then she leaned back in her chair to relax. John had been taking notes as he was listening, careful not to interrupt. But as she finished, he realized that her story was not complete.

Somewhat confused, he asked, "So where did they find her body?"

"Her body," she asked. Then she said as she looked down at the table, "But they haven't."

"What do you mean they haven't?" he asked.

She said, "They never did find her body. It's as though she just vanished."

Surprised, John said, "Vanished! Angelica, all you may have here is a missing person. She may be in Europe for all we know, not wanting to be found. She's probably somewhere, happily doing her artwork. As a matter of fact, you don't have any evidence to suggest that she was murdered."

"She's not in Europe. She's been murdered!" Angelica said with a sad yet determined tone.

John looked at Angelica. She seemed awfully sure of herself, which gave John an odd feeling. John asked as he leaned forward, "How do you know she's been murdered?"

"I just do," said Angelica. "Trust me!"

"Well, then why haven't any of her friends from the club that night come forward to talk to the authorities? Don't you think that they should have heard all this concerning Ken's behavior?" asked John.

"I guess they were just too afraid, considering the power of Ken's family," responded Angelica. Looking into her eyes, John began feeling extremely tired. Angelica suddenly rose up from the table, saying, "You look tired. Why don't you get a good night's sleep? I'll get in touch with you tomorrow."

John said, "I guess you're right. Can I get you a taxi or drive you somewhere?" He asked.

"No. That's okay. I'll make it on my own. I need you to sleep on what I told you, and I'll get in touch with you tomorrow," she said as she gathered her things and left the apartment.

As she left, John decided that he would read over some of his notes from her story, but he was so tired that he could barely keep his eyes open. Suddenly feeling extremely sleepy, he wandered into the bedroom. *What a day*, he thought as he collapsed on the bed. John, who usually slept on the couch in the living room, hadn't even realized that he was in his bed. He fell into bed for the first time in two years, and he began having an incredible dream.

CHAPTER 11

As John fell into a deep sleep, he began breathing heavily. It was as though the events that Angelica had described were racing through his mind. He began to see the events unfold as though he were watching a movie, visualizing her story from beginning to end. And then something unusual began to occur. His dream was taking him beyond the point where Angelica had stopped. It seemed as though her story was not yet finished. His dream began showing the events that took place where she had left off.

On the night that Susan disappeared, he was seeing her leave the nightclub alone. She seemed to be disturbed by the incident at the club between Ken and her. And to relax and get her mind off Ken, she decided to go to her studio. There she could work on her sculpture and forget her problems while listening to music. She drove to her studio and started working on her sculpture, and in his dream, he could see that she was a slender woman, looking similar to Angelica but not exactly.

Suddenly, she stood up as if she had been startled by something or someone. Looking frightened at first and then angry, he could see that she began to argue with someone who had apparently entered the room. Obviously, it was Ken. he must have followed her to the studio. As he approached, she began moving away from him. She reached down and picked up what looked like a sculpturing tool, and as he came closer, she began yelling, "Leave me alone, Ken. I don't love you anymore. Please just go away!" as she held out the tool to protect herself.

Ken's face became red with anger as she screamed those words. She could see that his eyes seemed to change in some way. He had this crazed infuriated look that reminded her of some crazed lunatic that only wanted to do her harm. This terrified her even more, and she knew that she had to get away. Suddenly, he made a lunging movement toward her. She quickly tried to run away, leaping back and around the corner of her sculpturing table. Sadly, as she pulled away from his clinches, she tripped and fell to the ground, letting out a deep moaning-type groan.

She was unable to get up and just lay there groaning in pain. Ken then ran over to her. His face began to change. It was as though he had snapped out of some evil trance and was now showing the look of a concerned lover. He reached down and rolled her over, discovering that the sculpturing tool had stabbed her in the stomach. He cradled her in his lap while rocking back and forth crying intensely.

She looked up at him with fear in her eyes as he pressed down on the wound with his hands. He tried desperately to stop the bleeding, but the wound was too severe. It wasn't long before she fell unconscious and soon thereafter stopped breathing. What happened next was even more disturbing in John's dream.

It seemed that after she died, Ken panicked, and not knowing what to do, he began looking around to see if anyone else was in the room. It was obvious that he was alone with Susan dead on the floor. He rushed over to the phone, picked it up, and started dialing. Hysterically, he began speaking to someone on the line. He hung up the phone and put his face in his hands. He stood there for a moment while standing over Susan.

Finally, after regaining control of his emotions, it looked as though he went to a back room in the studio returning with a large white sheet. He laid the sheet down on the floor next to Susan and rolled her limp body into the sheet. It wasn't long after that that another male who had short well-groomed red hair entered the room and immediately took control of the situation since Ken looked as though he was in no state to do so.

In John's dream, it looked as though Ken was trying to explain what had happened as the man with red hair began cleaning the bloodstained floor. This man was very thorough not to leave any evidence that Susan had even been there that night. With the floor clean, the two men focused their attention on the rest of the room, making sure that everything was in its place. They carried Susan's body wrapped in the sheet to the red-haired man's car, placing her gently in his trunk. The two men gathered all the blood-soaked items that they had used to clean up the place, including the sculpturing tool, and placed them in a black garbage bag. They then took the bag to the car and placed it in the trunk next to Susan.

The two men drove in separate cars to Ken's condo where they parked his BMW. Ken hurriedly got into the other car, and they drove back to Susan's studio, being careful not to get stopped or pulled over. Once they arrived, Ken jumped out of the car and got into Susan's car. Ken took off with the red-haired man following closely behind. In John's dream, it looked as though they drove into the parking lot of a grocery store and parked the car. It was late, and with the store closed, the two men carefully wiped off any fingerprints in or on Susan's car.

Then without saying a word, they got back into the red-haired man's car and drove away. They seemed to disappear in the darkness as John began to wake up.

As John awoke the next morning, he began remembering his dream. He was excited and immediately reached for his pad and pen so he could write them down. He thought to himself, *I think there's something to Angelica's story, and I think I may know what may have happened to Susan.*

With a new sense of enthusiasm, John couldn't wait to tell Angelica about his dream. He wanted to tell her immediately but had no idea how to get in touch with her. She hadn't left a phone number or an address or any information, so for now, he would have to wait.

John felt excited. He had a new attitude and a new sense of purpose. For the first time in two years, he felt good about the idea of being able to help someone. And having a new purpose in life would prove to be a new beginning for John.

Even though this woman named Angelica was a mystery to John, he knew that he might be able to help her in some way, realizing this gave John a feeling that he hadn't had in years—a sense of worth, a will to live, and a reason to go on.

Not wanting to wait at his apartment, John decided to go for a walk. It was early in the morning as John headed out, and the sun was just beginning to light the streets as he began his walk. Instead of taking his usual route, he decided to go the opposite direction. This new route would take him away from the grocery store where he normally went. It also took him away from the bar.

Instead, his new route took him past the church where he had had his confrontation with the priest. He stopped and took a long look at the church, but his feelings of guilt wouldn't allow him to enter. Suddenly, he could smell the fresh aroma of coffee. He walked down the street and around the corner to a small coffee shop where he stopped and bought a large coffee with cream and sugar as he continued on his way. He took in the sounds and smells that seemed to echo through the air.

He could smell the fresh pastry and hear the sounds of the birds chirping in the trees. He could hear a dog barking in a nearby park that somehow seemed to lure him in that direction. As he walked to the park, he noticed the squirrels scampering about as if they were playing for John's attention. He stopped and watched for a while before he smiled and went on his way, leaving the squirrels to themselves.

Noticing a bench near the playground area in the park, John decided to take a seat. He had been walking for about an hour, and the young children with their families were making their way to the park as well. Everything seemed to be coming to life around John as he sat on the bench, taking in all the activities. He realized how much he missed all the happiness in the world around him.

John thought, *I need to call Dex. He was always a good friend. He practically became a part of our family. Yeah. That's what I'll do.* With that thought, John got up and started on his way to find a pay phone. *Maybe we can meet at our old meeting place. He needs to meet Angelica anyway. He can probably help us on the case*, he thought to himself.

He had taken about two steps from the bench when he heard a young voice from behind him, saying, "Hey, mister." John stopped and turned around to look. He saw a young boy, about eight years old, running up with a football. The boy said again, "Hey, mister, can you throw me some passes?"

John stood there looking at the boy. He reminded him of his own son when he was about eight years old. How he loved to play catch with his dad, and John loved it as much as his son. His hair, his size, even the way he moved reminded him of his own son when he was about that age, and it was all too familiar in John's memories.

John's eyes began to water as he looked at the boy and said, "Sure, kid, I'll play some catch with you." The boy seemed delighted as John and he played catch. John had to fight back his emotions as he threw passes to the boy. It was all too familiar in John's mind as he realized that it had been over two years since he had last thrown passes with his own son. To John, it seemed like a lifetime ago.

Suddenly, he heard the voice of a young mother near the swings, calling to her son, telling him that it was time to go. The boy's name was Timmy, and John couldn't help watching him as he ran over to his mother where she was patiently waiting. The boy turned and looked back at John, shouting, "Maybe we can do this again sometime!" as he waved.

Full of emotion, John waved back as the boy walked away. Wiping off the tear from his cheek, John left the park in search of a pay phone to call his old friend Dex.

CHAPTER 12

John began walking home while thinking of the boy. He thoroughly enjoyed his time at the park, and he wished that he could have spent more time with the boy playing catch. But John, more than anyone, understood a mother's call to come home. *Maybe someday, I'll see him again*, he thought.

On his way home, John found a pay phone and called Dex. He wasn't at home, so he left a message asking him to meet at their usual place around five thirty that afternoon. Leaving that message for Dex gave John a feeling of excitement and rejuvenation that he hadn't felt in a long time. He thought, *What a surprise for Dex when he hears that message. Will he be shocked? Hopefully, he will be as excited as I am. I can't wait!*

It had been over two years since John had seen Dex, and he wondered if he had changed much. That's when he began feeling guilty because he had closed Dex out of his life for so long. "Hopefully he will understand," John said softly to himself as he continued to walk.

When John got home, he took a glance at his apartment and realized that it was a total mess. He immediately began cleaning up the place because he didn't want to be embarrassed again if anyone came over. As he cleaned, he noticed his alcohol sitting in its usual place. He slowly moved over to it and pulled it down from the top of the refrigerator. He then opened the refrigerator door and pulled out his beer. He stood over the alcohol, trying to decide if he should have a drink.

John looked down at his hands and waited. There was no trembling—none. He realized that he didn't have any symptoms of needing a drink. He raised his hands in the air and waited, just staring at his hands—nothing. He suddenly took the alcohol and quickly poured it all down the drain, saying to himself, "I can do this. I can. I can do this." John had no symptoms or desire for a drink as he spent most of that afternoon cleaning.

It was around 4:00 p.m. when he decided to focus his attention on himself. He entered his bathroom and looked in the mirror. Looking back was someone John didn't even recognize. *Who are you?* he thought. He dug out a razor that hadn't been used in a very long time. He grabbed a pair of scissors and started the process of removing the long shaggy beard that he had kept since his wife and children were killed. With every stroke of the razor, it was as though John was returning to his old self, slowly coming out of the dark, depressing world that he had been living for the past two years. But also, with every stroke of the razor and seeing himself in the mirror reminded him of that day, the horrible day that he lost his wife and children forever.

He stood there looking in the mirror and began wiping his clean face with his hands as if he was trying to wipe away his inner pain and his memories of that day. Sadly, those memories would not go away. He began to have an overwhelming urge to have a drink, and his hands began to tremble. "Who am I fooling?" he said as he stood there staring at himself in the mirror.

John turned and headed to the bedroom, saying, "I need to get to O'Mally's immediately." In a desperate attempt to mask his pain, he began frantically searching his apartment for the alcohol money that he would need.

Suddenly, he was startled by a knock at the door. With caution, he opened the door to see Angelica standing outside. Her beauty was remarkable, and as he looked deep into her eyes, she slowly smiled, giving John a calming feeling that began to take control of his emotions. The trembling in his hands began to subside, and his sudden desperate urge for a drink began to disappear.

She said softly, "Can I come in?" as she peeked around to see inside the apartment.

John moved aside, saying, "Sure. I've been waiting."

As she entered the apartment, she quickly looked around and said, "Well, we've been busy. It looks like you've been doing some housecleaning.

And your beard. You know, I prefer this look better. You look great!"

She entered the apartment with the same delicate grace and gentle walk that he had noticed last night. He couldn't help but watch her graceful movements as she moved through the apartment. It was as though she was a member of the English Royal Family, commanding the respect from all those who were around her. *What is it about this woman?* he thought to himself as he observed her moving into the living room area for a seat on the couch.

Then she asked, "So what do you think?"

John, startled by her question, responded as though he was coming out of some kind of trance, "Huh? What? What do I think? Oh, you mean your story." He began to gain control of his thoughts as he adjusted to the overwhelming charisma that she naturally projected. He said, "Funny thing happened after you left last night." He moved into the living room and sat on the opposite end of the couch. "That story you told me must have made an impact on me."

"Is that so?" she replied.

"Yeah. In fact, I couldn't get it out of my mind. I even had a dream about it," said John.

She began nodding and giving this look toward John that made him feel like she was expecting him to say that.

She said in a confident tone, "So you had a dream. Well, you know what they say."

John, looking confused, said, "No, I don't know. What do they say?"

"You should always listen to your dreams. They might be trying to tell you something," she replied.

"Well, I've never had a dream like this before. Let's just say that there might be something to this case and that I am interested enough to feel that I need to check some things out. Let's just see where things lead us," John said. "I hope you don't mind, but I called an old friend to help us with this thing. He's sort of an expert on research, and we could use his help."

Angelica said, "No, I don't mind. Whatever you think might be of help."

"Okay, then good because we're going to meet him at a coffee shop around five thirty this afternoon. Can you come?" asked John.

"I would love to," she replied. Angelica stood up and started walking toward the door. "I guess we better get going then. It's about fifteen till," she said.

John got up quickly from the couch and started toward the door. "Yeah, let's go. I'll drive. By the way, his name is Dex. I think you'll like him."

The two arrived at the coffee shop about ten minutes after five. They parked alongside the curb in precisely the same place that John had parked the last time that he was there over two years ago. An uneasy feeling came over John as he got out of the car.

He walked up and glanced around the corner where Nick and Telly had parked. It was as though he was looking for something or someone. This was where his nightmare had begun, and seeing this spot again made him wish that somehow he could take that day back. But he knew he couldn't, and as he took a deep breath, he turned to look for Angelica. To his surprise, she was headed in the other direction. "Hey, Angelica, the door's over here," he shouted. But she didn't stop.

John started to follow slowly as it looked as though she was approaching a homeless man sitting against the wall. John watched as she walked directly up to the man and offered her hand. *What in the world is she doing?* he thought. As the man reached up to take her hand, John shouted, "Angelica. Hey, Angelica." But she didn't respond.

The homeless man looked as though he had not eaten in some time. He was dirty with long stringy hair and seemed to be very listless. Angelica, showing no signs of fear, helped the man to his feet. John just watched as it looked like she started whispering to the man. The homeless man began to tremble, his eyes began to water, and then she gave him an embrace. John stood there watching in disbelief, not knowing what to do or say. She pushed him out at arm's length and with her hands on both his shoulders, continued her quiet conversation. The man was nodding his head as if he understood and then began wiping off his tears. She let go of his shoulders as he picked up his pack and coat and slowly started to walk away.

Angelica then turned to John and began walking toward the door of the coffee house. John wanted desperately to know what that was about, but he knew that that wasn't any of his business. She walked by John and went inside the coffee house without any explanation other than a simple smile. John followed Angelica inside, now more confused than ever as to who this mysterious woman really was.

He followed Angelica through the coffee house as she moved up to the table and sat down in her delicate and graceful manner. He noticed that she had drawn the attention of all the patrons. They seemed to be in a quiet hypnotic state as she moved past and sat down without giving any thought to the glances around her.

What was even more surprising or maybe just by coincidence was she sat down at John and Dex's regular seat, which was located at the window. She sat there with her back to the window. The evening light from the sun danced around her silhouette, making for an unusual effect. It seemed as though there was a glowing halo that was being projected around her image for everyone to see. John made his way to the table and quickly sat down. He looked at Angelica with a confused and curious look on his face.

John said, "That's amazing. You're amazing. Who are you anyway?"

"What's amazing?" she replied.

"That thing outside with the homeless guy. What was that about?" he asked.

She smiled at John and said in her typical soothing self, "John, let's just say I'm a lot like you. I like to help people if and whenever I can. Besides, HE likes that," as she gently pointed toward the ceiling.

John sat back in his chair and crossed his arms, showing signs of disbelief and even more confusion.

He then leaned toward Angelica from across the table and said in a soft quiet tone, "Give me a break. Are you for real?" He said with a teasing unsure laugh.

She responded by leaning in toward John and winking as she said softly, "If you believe. Do you? Do you believe, John?" She said as she pointed up.

A blank look came over John's face as he remembered those same words being said from the back seat of his car. He remembered the voices in his car that he had heard over two years ago on the night that he took care of Nick and Telly at Mystic Lake. Just then, Angelica stood up and said, "Can you excuse me for a moment? I need to go, well, you know."

John, in heavy thought, looked up at her and nodded that that was fine. She got up and slipped away. Just then, John looked up and saw Dex for the first time in over two years. A huge smile came across both men's faces.

Dex hurried over and without saying a word, gave John a hug. The two men stood there in a tight embrace for what seemed to be several minutes. With Angelica causing such a scene earlier, it wasn't difficult for John to suddenly realize that they were now the center of attention. Being somewhat macho men and extremely proud of their manhood, John cringed to think that all eyes were now on Dex and him. Now holding each other at arm's length, they couldn't help but look to confirm that, *yes*, Dex and he were in fact the center of everyone's attention. No one was saying a word. Instead, they all seemed to be giving a deep penetrating stare of disapproval. To make matters worse, it looked like every hardcore truck driver east of Chicago was in the place.

Dex and John, realizing what people must be thinking, pushed away from each other at precisely the same time, and in a loud deep voice for everyone to hear, John said, "Well, it's been a long time, Dex. How have you been doing?"

"Ye-Ye-Yes, i-i-it has. I-I-It sure has," Dex said as both men quickly sat down.

John leaned over to Dex from across the table and while shaking his head, said, "Well, I don't think your stuttering helped us out there, buddy!" as the two men began to laugh. "Dex, take a quick look. See if they've started chewing their food again," said John.

"I c-c-can't do it. Let's j-j-just ignore them," replied Dex.

The two men laughed for several minutes, and all seemed well between Dex and him. Apparently, there were no hard feelings with Dex. He, more than anyone, understood what John must have been going through the last two years.

Dex then looked at John and said in his usual stuttering self, "We-we-well, h-h-how have you b-b-been doing?"

"You wouldn't believe me if I told you, but it's been tough, very tough!" replied John. "You've been a good friend, Dex, and I'm sorry for disappearing the way I did. But I had to be alone for a while. I hope you understand."

The tone between the two men became more serious as each reflected the past two years in their minds. It had been a tough time on both, but neither was there to complain. They were just happy to see one another.

"I-I understand," replied Dex.

John said, "By the way, I called you here tonight to meet someone. She'll be back in a minute. She says she needs our help on a case."

Dex, looking somewhat surprised, said, "A case. Wa-wa-what kind of ca-ca-case?" asked Dex.

"I'll tell you all about the details later, but it's an old unsolved murder case," John replied.

"Mu-mu-murder!" said Dex as he seemed to get somewhat nervous. "B-B-but I'm not in law enf-f-f-forcement anymore."

"You're not. Well, what are you doing then?" asked John.

"U-U-Used cars. I'm selling u-u-used cars," replied Dex with an embarrassing grin.

Upon hearing Dex's new career, John threw his head back and began to laugh uncontrollably. Dex didn't seem to mind his laughing and actually joined in on his festive laughter.

John looked at Dex and said, "SALES. Now that takes it. I would love to come buy a ca-ca-car from you," as they continued to laugh.

"We-we-well, I wasn't v-v-very good," Dex replied. "I ga-ga-guess I ca-ca-can help."

John said, "Good. We got to get you out of s-s-sales and back into something you do well."

The two men sat across each other talking over old times until finally, John began to wonder what was keeping Angelica so long.

John then leaned over to Dex and with a more serious look on his face, asked in a soft whisper, "Are you very religious, Dex?" as he raised an eyebrow.

"As much as a-a-anybody I g-g-guess," he replied.

John looked around to make sure that no one was overhearing and asked, "Do you believe?" He asked quietly. Then again, he asked, "Do you believe in angels?" while squinting. Dex responded with his own chuckle, making John feel a bit silly for even asking the question.

"A-A-Angels!" Dex replied. "Why do you a-a-ask?"

"I know. I know. Just forget I even asked. It's just too far-fetched to believe," John said.

Before Dex could elaborate any further about the angel question, Angelica arrived at the table. Dex looked up at the beautiful woman and like everyone else, was in awe of her remarkable beauty. He was speechless and could only rise up from his chair to offer her a place to sit.

She said in her delicate voice, "Sorry it took me so long. I hope neither of you minded." Dex just stood there staring at Angelica as she offered him her hand. He slowly reached out and took it as she said, "I'm Angelica. You must be Dex."

He nodded, still staring into her eyes, and said, "Yes, ma'am, I am."

Suddenly, Dex realized that he didn't stutter. He spoke those four words clearly, confidently, and without hesitation. His eyes grew wide with joy as he reached for his throat.

She smiled and John asked, "Dex, are you all right?"

"I think so," he replied as he took a big gulp.

John realized as well that his old friend who had had a stuttering problem his entire life suddenly didn't. The two men looked at each other in astonishment as Angelica sat down.

Nothing was said of the miracle that had just occurred. What does one say? For Dex, it really was a miracle, for only those who have suffered the internal frustration and pain associated with having a stuttering affliction could understand. He kept his joy inside, though he wanted to scream with delight.

John and Dex knew that this was a very special lady if you could call her that. She was more like heaven-sent. And John, after witnessing several unusual events that had taken place in her presence, knew that she was here for a reason. He knew now more than ever that she needed his help, and he was determined to do anything he could to give her the help that she needed. The three sat at the table getting to know one another.

Dex struggled to hold back his tears of joy as she and John supplied him with information about the case. John included the dream that he had had from the night before as Angelica listened intently. She seemed to be nodding with every detail of his dream as if she was making sure that he was getting it right.

As he finished, she asked, "So what do you think? Can you help me?"

John said, "I hope so. It's an old case, but I think we can," as Dex agreed. He then said, "If we can just find out who this red-haired guy is or if he even exists, then I think that we may be on the right track."

Angelica quickly responded by saying, "I know who the red-haired guy is."

"Really. Who?" asked John.

She said, "That would be Ron, Kenneth's best friend. They both moved to Denver, Colorado, shortly after passing the bar exam."

"That's great, then this guy really does exist. Do you know where we can get a picture of this guy?" he asked.

"No, I don't," said Angelica.

Dex said confidently, "I can get it. I can get a picture of anybody."

Angelica began to grin, sitting quietly at the table and observing the two as they seemed to take charge and devise a plan of action.

John slapped his hands down on the table and said, "Okay, then it looks like we're off to Colorado!"

The three agreed that they would catch a flight out the next day headed for Denver.

Then Angelica began showing signs of hesitation and said, "Maybe I'll meet you two there." John and Dex looked a bit puzzled. "Besides, it will give you two a chance to catch up. I will meet you tomorrow at a place called the Rustic Woods Lodge and Resort, just northwest of Denver. It's an old fishing resort off Highway 36. Okay?" The two men agreed. As she got up from the table, she said, "I must apologize, but I have to leave. I need to be somewhere. Don't forget Rustic Woods Resort off Highway 36."

As she started to walk away, John said quickly, "Wait. I'll give you a ride."

"No, that's okay. I'll see you two tomorrow," she replied and quickly left the coffee house.

The two men watched as she left, not knowing what had just happened or why she had to leave so suddenly. They both were a bit mystified by Angelica and sat at the table waiting for the other to speak first.

Suddenly, a slow grin began to appear on each of their faces as Dex leaned over the table and said in a soft voice, "You know that question you asked me earlier, you know, about being religious and believing in angels."

John said, "Yeah," as he nodded.

"Well, I do now!" said Dex.

CHAPTER 13

After the departure of Angelica, John and Dex were able to catch up on things that had occurred over the past two years. Neither discussed all the problems that each had faced, deciding instead to keep some things to themselves. John especially wasn't very proud of the offenses that he had committed against Nick and Telly and wanted to avoid that whole conversation completely. Dex, however, had an idea of what John had done and decided not to probe John with what really happened. It seemed that they had a mutual understanding not to discuss the past from that moment on. John, on the other hand, was excited about Dex's newfound ability for gab.

During their conversations, he realized that Dex was quite intellectual. Sadly for Dex, however, he had been typecast because of his stuttering. Most people assumed that he was slow when, in fact, just the opposite was the case. John listened intensely as Dex demonstrated his remarkable knowledge of many topics. He seemed to be a walking and now talking encyclopedia. In fact, he had some sort of understanding on just about any subject that John could think of and then some.

John, being extremely impressed, said, "Dex, I'm sorry to interrupt, but, man, you need to be a contestant on *Jeopardy!* or *Who Wants to Be a Millionaire*. I never realized how smart you are."

"Well, it's always been a struggle for me to communicate, so frustrating and so embarrassing," he said as his eyes began to water. "You can't imagine what it's like to be laughed at and hear someone call you stupid under his breath, thinking I couldn't hear him. So I know what you're saying when you say you never realized how smart I am. I understand how easy it is to make that mistake."

John watched and listened to Dex as he described his innermost pain. He felt guilty as he, too, had laughed and made the remarks that Dex had described.

He felt very ashamed as he looked into Dex's hurting eyes but then Dex began showing signs of a small smile inching upward from the corners of his mouth as he continued, "Our society looks at people with a stuttering problem as being stupid or slow. But that's their stupidity. I knew a teacher who said that some of the brightest kids in her class were those with a stuttering affliction. Isn't that something?" He said as he smiled. "John, you're the only one who gave me a chance, and you're the only one who believed in my abilities to do my job. You have no idea how everyone blamed me for the death of your family. I even blamed myself. After all, it was my friend and my lead that lead us to the docks that night," Dex said as he hung his head.

John began to frown with sadness as he realized that Dex had been blaming himself for the horrific deaths of his loved ones.

"Dex, I never realized how painful it must have been for you over the past two years. I had no idea that you were going through this kind of guilt regarding my loss. I was too busy living in my own self-pity to even realize that you were hurting as well. I blame myself, Dex, not you. I had a chance to adhere to their warning, but I didn't. For that, I will never forgive myself. My pride and determination wouldn't allow me to recognize that my career had put my family at risk. That mistake cost my dearest loved ones, my innocent wife and babies, their lives. I will never forgive myself," John said as his voice began to weaken with emotion.

Dex reached across the table and touched John on the sleeve of his shirt, saying, "But, John, it was my lead, my mistake that sent us to the docks that night. I should have checked it out better. I should have been more thorough before I told you about that lead."

"You were just doing your job the same as I would have," responded John. "I'm the one that should have realized what was happening, but I didn't."

Both men grew quiet, neither knowing how to console the other or what to say. They would both quietly blame themselves and live with their own personal guilt forever. In some way, this seemed to create a bond between the two men that would endure the rest of their lives. John took a long slow gulp of freshly poured coffee. In some way, coffee seemed to make his troubles make more sense or ease his mind.

He returned the cup to the table and looked up at Dex, saying, "Dex, I need to say something," as Dex looked up.

"Yeah. What?"

"It's a sensitive issue. It's regarding your stuttering," replied John.

"No, that's okay. We don't have to," responded Dex as he shook his head.

"No, I know, but I feel I need to," said John as he looked away.

"You're right. Our society has become a less forgiving, sometimes even cruel society. You've really opened my eyes. I wished I knew what to say, but I don't, other than I'm sorry," replied John.

Dex grinned and said, "That's okay. John, it's just the way things are. You can either let it bring you down, making you a bitter person. Or you can use it to make you stronger and become a better person. Personally, I choose the latter of the two."

The two men digested their conversation as they sipped their coffee. Neither wanted to elaborate any further about their problems, so they sat quietly for a few moments, not saying a word. John had a new understanding of Dex and how difficult life had been for the both of them. But especially he appreciated his empathy and intelligence. It was amazing to

John how Dex could displace himself from himself and understand how people perceived him from their point of view. John realized through Dex just how cruel people can be and how quick society is to judge based purely on a handicap. *Never again*, he thought. *Never again*.

Anxious to change the subject, John asked Dex if he could borrow his cell phone to call the airlines. They had to book a flight to Denver before it got any later if they were going to get a flight out. Fortunately for them, it wasn't a particularly busy time of the year for travel, so they were able to book their flight with little problem.

John said, "I'll meet you at the airport at ten thirty in the morning. And I guess we'll meet Angelica at the lodge that she spoke about in Denver. What was the name again—Rustic Woods or something?"

"Yeah, it's called Rustic Woods Resort. She said it was located just outside Denver to the northwest. By the way, John, don't you think it's a little odd that she already had a place to meet in Colorado? It's as though she already knew we were going to go there!" said Dex.

"Dex, does anything seem to make sense about Angelica? After what I've seen, well, I just don't ask or question anymore. After all, you don't stutter anymore. Explain that!" replied John as Dex agreed.

Suddenly and unexplainably, a cold chill ran through both men as they thought of Angelica. They both shivered and noticed intense goosebumps on their arms. It was warm and comfortable inside the coffee house, so there wasn't any reason for the sudden chill. John called the waitress over to the table and asked if they had lowered the temperature. She responded politely and said no that they hadn't, but she did notice that at their table, it did feel uncomfortably cold. She waved her hands over and around their area so she could feel the change in temperature. "That's strange. It just seems to be right here," she said, looking a bit confused.

Dex and John looked at each other and at the same time, said, "I think it's time to go." Neither man wanted to hang around to see what might happen next, so they paid their bill and hurried out the door. Both men realized how late it was and decided to head home. They wanted to be rested for their trip, and both were excited about going to Denver.

It had been good seeing each other at the old coffee shop where they had always met to discuss a case. Memories had come flooding back to both men as they reminisced about better and happier times. As John reached home and entered his apartment, he looked over at the area where he had always kept his alcohol.

He hesitated and then shook his head as if to say he had no desire for a drink on this night. So he turned and walked away, heading for his bedroom. John seemed to have a new feeling of strength and confidence as he settled in for the evening. Relaxed and with his mind at ease, he fell into a deep and peaceful sleep.

Up early the next morning, John felt rested and was excited about his trip. He packed his luggage and headed off to catch his flight. When John arrived at the airport, Dex was already there waiting. He seemed to be as excited as John.

The flight was smooth and uneventful with the exception of Dex's constant craving for a good conversation. It seemed that he was making up for lost time with his new vocal abilities. Anyone and everyone within hearing distance could be a target. John enjoyed watching Dex move from one person to another, simply striking up a quick or sometimes lengthy conversation. The topic didn't seem to make a difference. Dex just wanted to talk.

The plane was relatively empty with plenty of seating available for those who wanted to move around. John watched as Dex made his rounds, wearing out one person after the other with unending conversations about whatever. As one person became disinterested, he would simply move to another. John started to stop Dex and tell him that he was beginning to annoy people, but John was having too much fun watching.

What was even more amusing to John was seeing how people quickly were able to come up with a solution to their tyranny at the sight of Dex's approach. Some would quickly immerse themselves in some sort of reading. Some were fortunate enough to have a book that they had brought on board. While others quickly and desperately seemed to be scrambling for anything to read. Usually, it was the material found in the back of the chairs. John looked back to see that most were holding up the proper instructions on how to wear your seat belt in front of their faces to avoid eye contact with Dex. Others simply rolled to the side and pretended to be asleep.

Dex, now with no one to talk to, had a sad, pouty, schoolboy look on his face as he sat, waiting patiently for someone to wake up. It was all John could do to hold back his laughter. Suddenly, he realized that Dex was heading in his direction. Like everyone else, John quickly leaned his chair back, rolled to the side, and pretended to fall asleep. *Poor Dex*, he thought as he silently laughed to himself. *He's now become a conversational nuisance.*

The plane landed and taxied up to the gate. John peeked to see that most of the passengers were still asleep or in more accurate words, pretending to be. Once the plane rolled to a stop, it seemed everyone woke up at the same time, jumped up, and quickly grabbed their personal items, leaving the plane as quickly as possible. Dex, when noticing that the people on board had awakened, had a look of joy compared to the look of a young child on Christmas morning. But he was quickly disappointed to see the sudden abruptness of everyone's departure.

John looked at Dex while still in their seats and said as he stretched, "Man, I slept great!"

"Well, it looks like everyone else did too," replied a frustrated Dex.

John began to laugh as the two gathered their carry-on items and left the plane.

"What's so funny?" asked Dex.

"Nothing. I'll tell you later," replied John.

As the two men made their way to the luggage-return area, the crowds that surrounded the terminal seemed to open up and part, allowing John and Dex plenty of room for easy luggage retrieval. Then they headed over to the rental car area.

Dex said, "That was strange. It was as though they were stepping aside, allowing us to get our luggage first."

John laughed and said, "Yeah, It was. In fact, it reminded me of Moses when he parted the sea."

Dex had a strange look on his face as he realized that he had probably been talking too much and that people were just avoiding him.

He said, "Okay. Okay, I get it. Why didn't you say something?"

John began to laugh hysterically, having to stop and bend over because his sides were cramping. John said, "I started to but then I couldn't. I was having too much fun."

As the two walked along, Dex kept repeating over and over, saying, "I can't believe you didn't say something. You should have told me," as John continued to laugh.

The two men picked up their rental car and a map of the local area. Soon, they were on their way to find the Rustic Woods Resort somewhere northwest of Denver. Just where, they weren't sure, but they knew that they had to get there and meet Angelica.

CHAPTER 14

It was cold and windy in Denver; obviously, a cold front was moving into the area. They headed north of the airport, hoping to find someone who knew the directions to the resort.

John asked in a loud aggravated tone, "Somewhere northwest of Denver. Dex, did she give any additional information to help locate this place?"

"Like what?" asked Dex.

"Well, let's see, specifically, maybe DIRECTIONS," yelled John as he rolled his eyes.

Neither man knew exactly where they were going other than they needed to get to the northwest of Denver. As they drove, they heard on the radio that the first snowstorm of the year would be coming that night. A weather advisory was posted, saying to expect eight to ten inches of the white stuff by morning. It was now about four in the afternoon, and the wind was becoming colder with every passing hour. Dex was able to locate on the map the main road that seemed to be heading to the northwest out of Denver. They felt that this road had to be the one that would take them to the resort.

"What's the highway number?" asked John.

"Looks like Highway 36," said Dex. "That's it. I remember. She said specifically Highway 36."

"All right. I knew you would come through. By the way, I am starving. You want to stop and eat?" asked John.

"That sounds great!"

They felt confident that they were headed in the right direction, and as they were leaving the Denver metroplex, they could see the winter storm on the horizon. With the help of their map, they were able to locate Highway 36 with relative ease. The road seemed to be a treacherous one, to say the least. It was a small two-lane road that seemed to be carved and cut through the mountain. Up and up, they traveled, following the twisting, winding steep road as if they were entering a new unseen and unexplored land.

"Dex, this is just beautiful country," announced John as he was looking around at the scenic view.

"I'll look. You keep yu-yu-your eyes on the road," yelled Dex.

"Dex, are we worried?" John asked.

"I sure would hate to go over the edge," he replied nervously.

On one side of the road was the mountain with no noticeable shoulder. On the other side was nothing but air. They had climbed in altitude rapidly and had traveled for about an hour. Dex could notice John clinching the steering wheel, which made him even more nervous than he already was. Neither man was talking at this point but was seemingly holding their breath, waiting anxiously to get off the nightmarish road that they had found themselves on.

"Are you sure we're on the right road?" asked John.

"I'm not sure of anything right now," said Dex nervously.

"Well, check the map!" said John as he, too, was becoming nervous.

Suddenly, the road went up and over a steep hill and then dropped down into what seemed to be a peaceful-looking valley. They were surrounded by mountains whose tops were white with snow. The two admired their surroundings as they made their descent to the valley floor.

"Thank god that's over with!" shouted Dex.

"Yeah, I'm with you on that," replied John.

Both men took a deep sigh of relief as they realized their treacherous journey was over for now. As they continued to drop down into the valley, John noticed that they were approaching a road sign.

"What's that say? What road are we on?" asked John.

"Let me see. Looks like Rustic Timbers Road. How did we get on that road? What happened to Highway 36?" asked Dex.

"I don't know, but let's stop at this restaurant up ahead. We can find out where we are and eat at the same time," said John.

Dex agreed as he began looking for Rustic Timbers Road on the map.

"It's not here. It's not anywhere on the map," Dex said with a puzzled look.

They pulled into the gravel-covered parking lot of the restaurant. It was an old rough-looking log-cabin-style structure. The name of the place was called The Country Griddle, and it looked about as rural as the store at Mystic Lake.

"How's this place look?" asked John with a smile.

"Old. Very old," replied Dex with displeasure.

They knew that they didn't have any other choice, so reluctantly, the two slowly got out of their car and looked around. There was a huge stack of firewood on the side of the building, stacked as if they were preparing for a long cold winter. John took a deep breath, taking in the smells of the clean mountain air. It was mixed with the presence of pine trees and burning wood from the fireplace.

He could hear the sounds of trickling water from a nearby creek and the echoes of the wind blowing through the treetops. Next door to the restaurant was a horse rental business. The horses showed signs of being unusually excited. They were jumping and kicking about the stall with an occasional high-pitched whinny that pierced the mountain air. John stood by his car, taking in all sounds and scenes around him as Dex began to shake from the cold mountain air.

He looked over at Dex and said with a smile, "This is great. I've never been to Colorado, but I think I could live here," as he took another deep breath.

Dex said, "Well, I couldn't. I'm freezing," as he began rubbing his arms.

"No, really, I could live here," John said again.

"Yeah, sure. Let's wait and see how you feel after about eight to ten inches of snow, and the temperature is about zero degrees," said a quivering Dex.

"We've got this kind of cold back home in Boston. This isn't anything unusual!" replied John.

"Not this kind of cold. This is different. This is a deep-feeling cold, a kind of cold-to-the-bones cold. Does that make sense?" asked a quivering Dex.

"Sounds to me like your catching the flu or something."

"I don't think so. I'm just cold," replied Dex.

John just smiled back as the two made their way into the restaurant. It was an old place with a huge fireplace and roaring fire located directly in the center of the room. As they entered, they could immediately feel the heat from the fire. They noticed that it made a warm, cozy climate inside. As they waited to be seated, an old underweight, unhealthy-looking woman stood by the bar watching the two, not saying a word or offering any guidance toward a table.

Finally, after what seemed to be an uncomfortable ten minutes, she walked up and said with an irritated tone, "Well, what is it?"

"We just wanted to sit down," replied John.

"Well, great, you can't sit down unless you're going to eat!" she said with an annoyed look.

"Oh yeah, well, we're going to eat. We're starving," said Dex.

"Well, then sit down where you want to. We aren't picky around here," she said with an attitude.

She stood there, staring at the two with a some-what-impatient look on her face as they began moving around the restaurant. Dex finally sat down at a table next to the fireplace to shake off his deep-felt chill. John, however, hesitated before sitting down. He preferred a window seat so that he could watch the sun drop behind the mountains. The mountains, which completely surrounded the valley seemed to create a bowl effect. The magnitude of their heights and their snowy white peaks made an incredible sight to see. It was a view that John had never been fortunate enough to observe before, and he wanted to take it all in.

However, Dex had already sat down, so John reluctantly sat down as well. The lady then approached the table and gave each a menu. She said, "I wouldn't sit there if I were you."

The two men on hearing that looked at each other and wondered, *What is it now?* They looked up at the old lady and noticed that she had a very serious look on her face and glaring eyes. Dex quickly looked around the dark room and realized that John and he were the only customers in the place.

Dex said, "Why not? Is this taken?" as he began to chuckle.

"No, it's not taken," she replied sarcastically.

She stood over the table, waiting for the two to get up and move, but they didn't. John and Dex sat there, waiting for her to continue her remarks as to why they needed to move, but she didn't. For what was an uncomfortable minute or two, no one said a word while each waited for the other to respond. Finally, she said, "Okay, have it your way then," as she walked away. John and Dex looked at each other, both feeling somewhat bewildered at the old lady's attitude.

John leaned over and whispered to Dex, "I wonder what that was about."

"I think that she may be going through menopause," replied Dex. "You know that cranky attitude. Yup, typical menopause behavior!" he said as he rolled his eyes.

"Menopause!" laughed John. "By the looks of her, I think she's well beyond that stage. Maybe an increase in her hormone prescription. That would probably help immensely."

The two men sat at the table and began to laugh loudly as they tried to figure out the old lady's behavior. Suddenly, their own laughter was interrupted by the sounds of heavy laughing coming from the back room of the restaurant. John and Dex looked at each other as they listened to the nonstop and hysterical sounds of people laughing. The echoing sounds made John and Dex feel even more uncomfortable than they already were. As the sounds stopped, a door flew open from the rear of the restaurant.

In walked a large muscular man carrying an arm load of giant logs. He had a smile on his face as he walked past John and Dex. Without saying a word, he stopped for an instant, giving him enough time to throw his wood onto the fire. He then turned, winked, and walked off, exiting through the doors from which he came. Then the laughter started again.

"Who was that Paul Bunyon?" asked Dex.

"I don't know, but he was huge," replied John.

Dex said, "Well, it sure was nice of him to put more wood on the fire for us. Maybe I can get rid of this chill," as he kept rubbing his arms.

"You must be getting sick or something because this fire is starting to really put out some heat," John said as he moved his chair away from the fireplace.

Both men began concentrating on their menu to determine what to eat. John could still hear the constant laughter from the back and took a second to look around but found nothing unusual. They must be having a party in the back he thought to himself.

The fire began to blaze higher and higher, putting out an intense heat as the two men continued to focus on their menu. John suddenly realized that they were sitting much too close to the fire and started to say something to Dex about moving to another table. Suddenly, Dex let out a scream, jumped up from the table, and took off running about the room, screaming, "Help! Help! I'm on fire! I'm on FIRE! Help!" while grabbing at his back.

John jumped up and grabbed a nearby pitcher of ice water and began chasing Dex while yelling for him to stop. He then poured the near-frozen cold water on Dex, which gave him an immediate feeling of relief.

John then quickly looked Dex over and said, "You're not on fire. I don't see any burned spots, and nothing seems to be smoking," as he looked at his clothing.

"Are you sure? I felt like I was on fire," Dex said, panting heavily.

About then, John and Dex could hear even more intense laughter coming from the back of the place. They looked at each other and realized that they had been set up by the people who ran the establishment.

John said, "Next time someone tells us to move, let's move!" as Dex agreed.

"By the way, are you sure I'm not burning somewhere?" asked Dex as he looked over his clothing.

"No, I'm sure. Come on. Let's sit over by the window," replied John as he walked over to the table.

The old lady walked out from the back, carrying a notepad. As she came nearer to the table, Dex could see that she now sported a hefty grin on her face. Her eyes were red and watery, which were basic signs of someone who had been laughing uncontrollably. As soon as she came up to the table, her smile disappeared, and she returned to her earlier gruff self. The old lady quickly took their order and left as the owner of the restaurant walked up and introduced himself. His name was Rick Parker and was the same man who had thrown the heaping pile of wood on the fire earlier. Both Dex and John were leery of the man as he approached, wondering just what he had in store next for everyone's entertainment. However, he turned out to be a quite pleasant individual, just guilty of having an extreme sense of humor.

He said, "I'm sorry about that," as he laughed. "I couldn't help myself. I knew you guys were not from around here, and we just wanted to have some fun. I hope you didn't take offense."

"Oh no. No, we're fine," responded John and Dex almost at the same time.

Dex said, "You know that can be pretty dangerous. You could really catch someone on fire!"

"Well, let's see. No, we've never actually had anyone burst into flames. Well, actually, there was this one guy, but you don't want to hear that story," Rick said with a serious, almost-crazed look on his face.

Dex and John glared back at Rick without saying a word. Dex had horrific thoughts, wondering if these people were some backwoods-crazed killers who would take joy in first torturing their victims before killing and mutilating their bodies. He seemed to be most disturbed by Rick's quiet stare. He actually had scenes from the movie *The Texas Chain Saw Massacre* running through his mind at high speed. Dex had almost reached the point where he was ready to leap from the table and run out the door when both John and Rick began to laugh, easing Dex's fear for the time being. What John didn't realize was that Dex had good reason to be fearful of Rick and the old lady and that this night would mark the beginning of some strange and unexplainable events that would affect their lives forever.

CHAPTER 15

The weather was getting worse outside as the cold front made its way into the area. With the temperature dropping, John noticed that the windows in the restaurant began to show signs of ice accumulating on the outside. As the sun disappeared behind the mountaintops, extreme darkness began to fall throughout the region, making an eerie, cold, dark night. Darkness also began to quickly fill the inside of the restaurant, making it difficult to see anything that wasn't near the glow of the fireplace.

As John's and Dex's food arrived, Rick, the restaurant owner, said, "I hope you enjoy your meal. I need to get some light going before it gets any darker in this place." He then leaned over the table to take a look outside and said, "Looks like it's going to be one of those black nights."

"Black nights. What's that?" asked Dex.

Rick slowly looked over at Dex as he leaned over the table and said in a soft eerie tone, "Cold pitch-black kind of night. If I were you, I would stay inside tonight. Strange things always seem to happen on these kinds of nights. Either stay inside or get out of this valley as fast as you can."

He suddenly pushed back from the table, turned away, and headed toward the back of the restaurant. Dex, already nervous about being in the place, couldn't help but watch Rick as he walked away from the table. To Dex's amazement, it seemed as though Rick simply disappeared in the dark as though he just faded out of sight.

"Did you see that?" asked Dex.

"See what?" asked John.

"It was like he vanished in the dark as he walked away," said a nervous and excited Dex.

"Dex, lighten up. They're pulling your leg. That stuff about a cold black night, they're just trying to scare you," replied John.

"Well, it's working, but really, it looked like he vanished," said Dex as he began to look back over his shoulders.

John looked at Dex and grinned, then he began to eat his meal. They had each ordered the house special, which was chicken fried steak. Neither man had ever eaten a real chicken fried steak before, and both were delighted how good it was.

As the two men began enjoying their meal and Dex started to finally relax enough to eat, Rick and the old lady suddenly appeared from nowhere, lighting candles throughout the restaurant. John continued to eat his meal as Dex observed the two shuffling about from candle to candle. Dex noticed that with the lighting of each candle, a new life began to emerge from inside the restaurant. Shadows began to dance on the walls in some weird inconsistent pattern almost as though they had a life of their own.

Even stranger than that was the way Rick and the old lady began to appear as they moved throughout the room against the soft amber glow of the candles. Dex could only sit and watch as the two made their way around the room. He realized that something seemed different about the pair. *Is that my imagination?* he thought as he took a harder look at the two. He was reluctant to say anything to John at this point, for he knew that John already thought he was paranoid, so he sat quietly and observed.

The old lady finally came closer, allowing Dex to get a more detailed look. To his dismay, he realized that what he thought he was seeing was in fact real. "Their bones. I can see their bones," he said softly to himself as his mouth dropped and his eyes grew wide with disbelief. Frozen in his chair with fear, he could only sit and stare. Their skin seemed to be transparent while their bones were looking luminescent in the strange amber lighting that filled the room.

Dex began tapping on the table to get John's attention while pointing and saying over and over, "Their bones. Their bones. I can see their bones," in a soft voice.

John looked up at Dex and noticed that he had a strange, disturbed look on his face. He asked, "What is it, Dex?" as he looked over where Dex was pointing.

"Their bones. I can see their bones," he responded.

"What? Their bones?" replied John as he turned to take a look for himself.

As John turned to see what Dex was talking about, Rick and the old lady disappeared in the back of the restaurant. Confused, he then looked back at Dex to see that he was extremely shaken by something.

John said, "Man, you've got to get ahold of yourself."

"But I could see their bones in their hands, their arms, and even in their faces," replied an excited Dex.

"Come on. You're just seeing things. It's been a long day. You're probably just tired," said John.

"No. Really, I could clearly see their bones as they were walking around here lighting candles," replied Dex.

John could tell by the look on Dex's face that he was serious and was desperate for John to believe what he was saying. This made John feel a bit nervous himself when suddenly and without warning, Rick came up to the table from out of the dark background of the room. Both men jumped in their seats and let out a high-pitched screech as Rick quickly appeared.

"Are you enjoying your meal?" he asked.

As John tried to catch his breath, Dex took a big gulp. "Oh yeah. In fact, I think we're finished eating," replied John.

"Well, I'll get your plates for ya then. By the way, are you two here to meet Angelica?" Rick asked.

"Yeah, we sure are. How do you know her?" responded a curious John.

"She was here earlier. In fact, she's already checked in. She even had me reserve a place for you two," said Rick.

"I'm not sure I understand. Is this the Rustic Woods Resort?"

"Yeah, this is it. The cabins and the lake are out back. In fact, I've got your keys to your room all ready to go. Your room is 12-C. It's the third set of cabins and the ones closest to the lake. We only had this one room available on such short notice. It has two double beds. You should be just fine," said Rick as he laid the keys on the table. "By the way, your meals are on the house," he said as he walked away laughing.

John and Dex were both a little astonished by all the events of the evening. The way everything had worked out and by stumbling their way onto this place was a bit weird, but everything about Angelica had been a bit weird.

The two were anxious to leave the restaurant, and as they stepped outside, they soon realized just how much the weather had changed in a very short time. The wind was extremely cold and wet with moisture accompanied by an unusual noise, like a howling voice. To John, the voicelike howl seemed to be familiar in its tone. Just as the two men made their way to the car, John suddenly stopped and stood silently, listening with an intense look on his face.

"What is it?" asked Dex.

"Can you hear that?" John replied.

Dex listened for a moment with the same intensity as John. "No. Hear what? I just hear the wind," responded a confused Dex.

"You can't hear that? It sounds like a young woman," said John.

"A young woman! What do you mean a young woman? What's she saying?"

John threw up his hands, motioning for Dex to be quiet as he listened again for the voice. Already on edge from the evening's previous events, Dex quickly jumped in the car and slammed the door as John remained outside. Dex watched on as John moved slowly and carefully around the car.

After a few moments, John finally thought that he could clearly understand what the voice was saying. He heard in a soft, weak, and desperate voice, "Help me. Help me. Please, help me." John began to turn in all directions trying to pinpoint where the voice was coming from. However, suddenly, it went away, leaving John with an empty feeling of helplessness and confusion.

He slowly got into the car and started up the engine. The two men were quiet as they were both in heavy thought of the evening's events. Neither was saying a word, and both were breathing rapidly, not knowing what to say. As they pulled away from the restaurant, the frost from their breath seemed to fill the car and accumulate on the windows. They began to make their way to the cabins, which were located in a dark low area behind the restaurant. John thought to himself, *Maybe it was just the wind that I was hearing after all.* And he tried to get it out of his mind. Suddenly, Dex got a strange and frightened look on his face, lunged for John, and grabbed him by the arm, screaming for him to look at the windows.

John hit the brakes as Dex continued frantically, "The windows. Look at the windows in the restaurant!"

"What? the windows," John asked as he looked.

"You didn't see them standing in the windows?" asked Dex.

"No, I don't see a thing," said John as he continued to look.

Dex's face was white with fear as he repeated himself, saying, "They were standing in the window, just watching us with these yellow-orange-looking glowing eyes!"

"Say what? Yellow eyes! What are you talking about?" asked John as he turned to take another look. "Well, I don't see a thing."

"You don't. Well, they were just standing in the window, watching. It looked like they were grinning with this weird, eerie grin. Man, let's get out of HERE!" shouted Dex.

"We can't drive out of this valley tonight, not with this kind of snow coming down. The radio said earlier we are supposed to get eight to ten inches tonight. I'm not about to try to drive out of here on that road. Are you crazy?" said John.

Dex said, "Crazy. Crazy. Ha. You're crazy for staying out here if you ask me. These people out here are crazy weird."

"Don't say it. I don't want to hear it," John said as he threw his hand up in Dex's mouth.

He wasn't ready to admit or even think about those two at the restaurant being of a ghostly sort, but they were very odd characters, to say the least. They pulled up in front of the cabins where they would be spending the night. As they parked and got out of the car, they noticed that a light was on in the cabin next to theirs. "Hopefully Angelica is in there," said John.

Dex looked around to see that all the other cabins were dark and abandoned-looking. The cabins seemed to be in a semicircle, facing the center of the complex, and in the center was an old-fashioned well that looked like it was from the eighteen hundreds.

"Yeah, I would say that that's probably her in there, especially by the looks of this place. This place is a run-down dump!" complained Dex.

"We must be the only ones here."

The snow was now coming down heavily with what looked like golf ball-sized snowflakes. They could almost hear them as they hit the ground. The ground around them was quickly turning to a beautiful white, but as they looked out away from the lights, it became cold and black. Just then, Dex remembered what Rick at the restaurant had said about a cold black night, and it suddenly seemed to make what he said all too real.

Dex said, "Hey, John, you remember what that guy said about the cold black-night stuff?"

"Yeah, I remember," answered John with no additional remarks.

"So what do you think now?" asked Dex.

John had no reply. It was as if for the first time since they arrived that he seemed to be concerned. The silence and lack of response didn't seem to help Dex relax either. In fact, it made him even more nervous than he already was.

"Let's get our stuff and get inside," John said with a more serious look on his face. The two men grabbed their luggage and made their way into the room. It was dark and very cold both inside and out.

Inside the cabin, they noticed an inviting fireplace with a big stack of logs ready to be burned. Dex immediately started building a fire as they heard a knock at the door. The two men stood frozen with a sudden surge of fear. The knock at the door was unexpected as they could only imagine what could happen next on this strange night.

John looked at Dex and quietly said, "Well, are you going to answer the door?" as he pointed.

Dex backed up and began shaking his head no. "I'm not answering the door. You do it."

John looked at Dex with disgust and then slowly crept over to the door, leaned over, and put his head on it as if to hear who or what may be on the other side.

Suddenly, a loud *bang, bang, bang* at the door, which sent John jumping backward and over the bed.

Then a soft voice from the other side, "John, are you and Dex all right?" To their relief, it was a familiar voice.

John opened the door to find Angelica standing there in a heavy white winter coat. She was looking as lovely as ever, and when she smiled, it seemed like all the troubles and fears they had experienced throughout the day disappeared.

CHAPTER 16

It was about seven forty-five that evening. The wind was howling outside and looked as though an all-out blizzard had arrived. The snow was coming down so hard that no one dared to go outside for fear of getting lost in the darkness. The visibility was minimal, and the snow was falling at a rate of about three to four inches an hour. Huge snowdrifts began to pile up along the sides of the cabins. The fire that Dex had built warmed the inside of their cabin, making a pleasant coziness that seemed in some way out of place, considering the conditions outside. Sitting in the corner of the room was an old wooden table. To Dex's delight, there sat a new and unused coffeepot with an unopened can of coffee nearby.

Dex said, "Great, we can make some coffee," as he hurried over and began brewing.

"You know, for a resort, you would think that they might have a TV or radio in this place. It's like we're totally isolated from the rest of society out here. What if something were to happen to one of us, and we needed help? I don't even see a phone."

"I'm sure they have a phone. It's probably in the lodge where we ate," replied John.

Angelica moved closer to Dex, seeming to try to help ease his mind and said in her usual soft, soothing voice, "Listen, guys, we're just fine out here, and everything is going to be okay. This storm will blow over, and all will be well in the morning. You'll see. I knew how much you both love coffee, so I picked these things up on my way out here. I thought it would make you both feel more comfortable."

John, who had been looking out of the window at the storm, had been feeling his own discomfort. He turned to listen to Angelica as she spoke. Her voice was soft and innocent yet strong and confident. She projected a soothing comfort that neither man could explain. As John listened, he, like Dex, began to feel more at ease.

He sat down in the chair that was under the window and said in his own confident tone, "Well, you know, you're right about that. A fresh pot of coffee will make us feel right at home." He said as he smiled, "Isn't that right, Dex?"

"Huh? Oh, yeah. Sure, it will," responded Dex.

"When I arrived in Denver this afternoon, I also picked up a local phone book before I came on out. I thought it might be useful," said Angelica.

"Yeah, but there is no phone," responded Dex.

"Like I said earlier, maybe there is a phone in the lodge that we can use," John replied.

"Well, then you can go up there. I'm not. Those two give me the creeps," said a frightened Dex.

"Okay. Okay, I'll go up there," John said as he rolled his eyes. John then turned his attention to

Angelica and said, "That's good thinking that you brought a phone book out here. We can see if Ron and Ken still live in the area. Maybe we can get their address and pay them a visit tomorrow, if we're not snowed in that is. By the way, Dex, did you manage to get a picture of this guy, Ron?"

"Yeah, I did. After I got home last night, I was able to pull up some information over the Internet on both Ron and Ken. It seems these two were pretty popular fellows in college. They were elected president and vice president of their fraternity. Of course, Ken was the president. I even managed to print a copy of their graduation pictures," Dex said as he sat back on the bed with a big smile on his face. "Here, let me get them for you. They're over here in my suitcase."

Dex got up and started digging through his bags as John and Angelica looked on. After a few minutes, Dex shouted out, "Finally, here you are," as he pulled out the pictures. John's face lit up with excitement when he heard the news. He moved over to Dex and anxiously waited to see the pictures. Angelica moved over as well; however, she seemed somewhat reluctant and nervous about something. John had never seen that in her before. She began to tremble as each picture appeared.

John noticed her sudden change in facial expression. It was obvious that seeing these pictures would bring back some deep heartfelt pain that only she was aware of. John couldn't help but watch the pain written on her face as the pictures materialized.

When Dex handed over the pictures and she saw them for the first time, her face cringed with disgust as she gazed. She took each picture and looked closely, standing quietly, just staring. She looked up at Dex and shook her head acknowledging that these were the two. Then she threw the picture of Ron down, and while holding the picture of Ken, she began to run her hands over Ken's picture. John and Dex didn't say a word but simply watched Angelica as she showed an emotion that they hadn't seen from her before.

John felt that he needed to break the tension, so he loudly asked Dex, "So, Dex, why didn't you tell me about these pictures earlier?"

"Are you kidding? With all that had been going on today, I haven't even thought about it until now," he replied.

"That's right," she said as she shook her head. "They were both in the same fraternity. Everyone had an unusually high respect for them. They were both considered untouchable as far as any investigation directed toward them regarding Susan. They both came from powerful families, especially Ken. I think that's what sickens me more than anything. It seems the investigators simply turned their backs. They didn't even bring them in for an interview," responded Angelica.

She slumped her head down to try to hide her emotions as John and Dex looked on. They could tell how much it meant to her to bring these two men to justice. However, neither man knew exactly what to say to soothe her pain. The room was quiet, and no one was saying a word.

Only John could see that a small, tiny tear began to trickle down on Angelica's cheek. He watched as it made its way down her face under her left eye. It had a strange sparkle that seemed unusually luminescent, much like the reflections of light beaming through a beautifully cut diamond. John didn't say a word nor could he take his eyes off it. Suddenly, it dropped from her cheek and began to descend toward the floor. It seemed to fall in a strange floating-like descent. Then it began to break apart into what looked like millions of tiny water particles that strangely seemed to float around the room. Each one produced the same brilliant tiny sparkle before fading out of sight. Only John seemed to notice the particles of water as he watched the tiny particles in amazement, and as they disappeared, he noticed that the room began to fill with a fragrance similar to jasmine.

Suddenly, the pleasant fragrance began to take on a new yet familiar aroma to John. This new fragrance in some way reminded him of his family. Each family member having his own unique scent that only a loved one could identify with began to rush through John's senses, reminding him of happier times.

John wanted so much to be able to find some of his family's clothing after they were killed that day. He wanted to press each article of clothing gently to his face and breathe in their own unique aroma, keeping their memories and faces in his mind, but the fire took that away as well.

For some time, John had been unable to picture his loved ones in his mind, but for some strange reason, this smell that now filled the room seemed to jar his memories, and for the first time in a while, he could see each one clearly. They were all together playing as they had so many times in the past. They were all smiling and playing in his backyard as though nothing had ever happened to them.

John closed his eyes so that he could somehow escape from his surroundings and enjoy the visions that were flooding into his mind. In some desperate way, he wanted the past two years to simply be a bad dream. How he wanted to reach out and hold them and tell them how much he missed them. His visions were suddenly interrupted by Dex tapping him on his shoulder. "Here, John. Here's your coffee."

Startled, John had a strange feeling come over him. He stood up and made his way to the window where he watched the falling snow. He wondered to himself, *Who is this person? What is this person? Could she really be an angel? No. I'm not sure I believe in angels or heaven or any of that stuff anymore. After what I've been through the last couple of years, no. God would never allow that kind of tragedy to happen to my beautiful wife and children. And if she is an angel, why would she be here? Why does she need my help? No, after you die, there is only a dark, cold hole that they stick you in and that's it, nothing else, but there has got to be a reason for all this weird stuff going on.*

Suddenly, the silence was broken by Angelica's soft-spoken voice, "I'm a lot like both of you. The two of you have spent your life helping people and that's what I spend my time doing, helping people. Only in this situation, I can't help Susan, but the two of you can help me bring these two men responsible for her disappearance to justice. That's why I am here. These two men were able to get away scot-free with virtually no change in their lives, except for their own conscience if they have one. Well, I'm here to change that, but I need your help to do it. I know that you both have questions and doubts, but in time, you will both have the answers that you need." Angelica spoke with a tone of confidence as John listened intensely to each word. *That's strange. It's like she read my mind*, he thought.

With a sudden grace-like quality, she then excused herself, saying, "I think tomorrow will be a big day. We all need to get some rest. I'll see you both in the morning." Angelica left the room and went next door as both men agreed that it had been a long and interesting day. John said, "She's right. Let's get some sleep."

They turned off the coffeepot and settled into their beds. With the storm and the howling wind echoing throughout the night, both men began feeling extremely uneasy. The wind was intense, and after the lights were turned out, it seemed that the sounds of the storm became magnified with an intensity unlike anything either of them had ever experienced before.

They lay in bed listening, each with his own nightmarish imagination running wild. They could hear the rustling of some kind of movement outside. At first, it sounded like metal trash cans being blown around by the wind, then an occasional and unexplainable loud pounding noise that made both men jump in their beds, followed by the sounds of someone walking on wooden planks that seemed to lead directly to their door. Both men clutched their sheets as they lay in their beds. What made things worse were the eerie loud thuds and dragging sounds that seemed to closely follow the footsteps. Neither one could sleep, and both were too embarrassed to admit that they were afraid, so they lay in bed quietly, listening to the haunting sounds of the storm.

CHAPTER 17

About thirty minutes had passed, and both men were still struggling to get to sleep. The storm was continuing its onslaught on the resort, and the occasional loud bangs and thuds made it impossible for either to relax.

Finally, Dex rose up and said in a frustrated tone, "Well, I can't go to sleep! Can you?" He asked. But there was no reply from John. "Hey. Hey, are you asleep?" he asked for a second time. But there was still no response from John. Dex then spoke a little louder with a new concerned sound in his voice. "Hey, John. John, are you asleep?" he said, waiting impatiently for a reply.

Finally, John rolled over and rose up in bed, turning toward Dex. "Dex, if you don't hear a response or see any kind of substantial movement, then the chances of me being asleep are pretty good. But no, I'm not asleep," replied a frustrated John as he lay back down in bed.

"Well, I can't go to sleep. I'm not even close to going to sleep!" said Dex. "All this weird stuff going on and those two at the restaurant, man, I'm like freaked."

"Yeah, I know. Just try to think about something else. Maybe that will help you fall asleep," replied John.

"Like what?" asked a nervous Dex.

"You know, anything. Try counting or something. That always helps me."

"Counting! You mean like counting sheep?"

"Well, sheep, ducks, anything. Just close your eyes and start counting."

"Does that really work?" asked Dex.

"Just try it!" he replied.

"All right, I'll try anything at this point," said Dex as he pulled the covers up over himself and rolled over.

Both men settled back down in bed. It wasn't long before John was almost asleep when he heard Dex for a second time.

"John. John," he said nervously.

"What? What is it now?" John asked.

"I started counting sheep like you suggested."

"Yeah!"

"Well, they turned into ghosts and then just skeletons all jumping over this fence, and as they jumped, they slowly turned their heads and looked right at me. Then they stopped and just stared at me, like those two in the window at the restaurant. Man, I can't sleep!" said a panicky Dex.

John sat up and, with this stunned look on his face, said, "Are you kidding? I did too. I saw the same exact thing."

"You did, really?" asked an excited Dex.

"No, I didn't. I'm just messing with you. Now please go to sleep," John said with a smile.

John settled in again and tried to go to sleep. As he lay there, he began to notice that the winds didn't seem to be blowing as hard outside. *Maybe the worst of this storm is over. I hope so. I'm exhausted,* he thought. He could hear Dex rolling and thrashing in the covers. He knew that Dex was struggling to get to sleep. *Poor Dex. He's just letting his imagination get the best of him, but I must admit, there is some weird stuff going on,* he thought.

After a few minutes, he could tell that Dex had become very still, and it wasn't long thereafter that he could hear Dex breathing heavily as though he finally got to sleep. That seemed to cause John to relax as well. He rolled over, took a deep relaxing breath, and sank deeply into his pillow.

He closed his eyes, and without warning and very softly in the far-off distance, he thought he heard that voice. It was the same distressed cry from earlier that evening. John opened his eyes and lay there, not moving a muscle, just waiting for it to return. He held his breath so that he could be sure that it was real and then there it was again. "Help me. Please, somebody help!" The voice was very faint, but it was clear.

John sat up slowly and looked over at Dex. He was sound asleep. That figures. Now that something was really happening, he was going to sleep through it. Then he heard faint whimpering. It was similar to the sounds of a little girl or a very young woman crying. John thought to himself, *I hope that everything is all right with Angelica. Maybe I need to go check on her and see.*

He got out of bed quietly so as not to wake Dex. He stumbled carefully about the dark room while putting on his clothes. He found his coat and was ready to make his way outside when suddenly, a deep chill ran through his body. It seemed to completely penetrate his entire being, almost as though this chill in some way had touched his soul. He stepped back and tried to make sense of this feeling that he had just felt when he heard a soft whispering voice. It was as though whoever was speaking was standing right next to him in this dark room.

The voice calmly said, "Do you believe, John? Do you believe?" John swung his hands and arms quickly in a circle around himself as though he were trying to locate the person that had just spoken to him, but there was nobody there. Then he heard the soft cry for help again coming from outside. The voice seemed different from the last. John was confused, but he knew that he had to check on Angelica.

He opened the door and stepped out into the cold night. John was breathing heavily with excitement, and his breath froze instantly upon contact with the night air. *Strange*, he thought. The snow was no longer falling, and there wasn't any wind, but there was an eerie quiet that seemed to overcome the valley.

Each step that he made in the snow seemed to make an uncomfortable crunching sound that penetrated the now-quiet night. He slowly made his way to Angelica's room where he put his ear to the door, listening for any familiar cries.

However, all was quiet. He turned around and looked out into the darkness toward the lake, waiting for something, some noise, anything, but nothing happened. "This is stupid!" he said out loud. "What am I doing out here? Man, now my imagination is getting the best of me. At least Dex is still in bed."

He started back to his room, and suddenly, the voice came back. John stopped instantly, frozen either with disbelief or fear, probably a little bit of both. The voice repeated itself, saying, "Please, somebody. Please help!"

John was able to determine that the voice seemed to be coming from the lake. *I hope no one has fallen in*, he thought. He started making his way toward the lake's edge. It was extremely cold, and he couldn't imagine that someone would actually be out in the water. It was dark, and the only light that could be seen in any direction was the light that hung over the water well, which was located in the center of the complex.

Suddenly, he heard the voice again. It seemed to be coming from somewhere out in the lake. John yelled out, "Hello. Where are you? Hello!" Then he heard a high-pitched scream and the sounds of someone splashing about in the water. It seemed like the sounds of some desperate struggle to survive. "Whoever it is, they need my help," he said to himself.

John quickly ran to his car and retrieved a flashlight. He made his way back to the lake's edge and began shining the flashlight over the water. The air was so cold that a thick dense fog rose up off the water, making it impossible to penetrate with the light. *This is no good. I can't see a thing*, John thought. Just then, he heard the cry for help again. *It sounds like she's just off the bank. But why can't I see her?* he said. He noticed a small boat at a nearby dock. He got in it carefully and began making his way out onto the cold dark water. John's heart was racing. He knew that there probably wouldn't be much time to help someone if they in fact fallen in the water.

He paddled for a while and then stopped to listen while shining the flashlight, hoping that he would get lucky and come across the struggling young woman. Occasionally, he heard her cry, but it was as though he wasn't getting any closer. He became frustrated and yelled out for her, but it seemed as though it wasn't doing any good. He thought to himself, *I must be halfway across this lake by now. I've been paddling for at least thirty minutes.* He slowly stood up in the middle of the boat. It was very wobbly, and he feared that he could easily tip over, but he felt like he had to try one last time to try to locate her. As he rose up from the seat of the boat, he could see that there was a glow in the water about fifty yards in front of him. *That's strange*, he thought.

He sat down slowly and began paddling. He could no longer hear the woman crying or splashing about in the water as he made his way toward the glowing water. After about five minutes, he came to the edge of the glow. It was a shade of luminescent turquoise blue resembling what is seen only in the tropics.

Suddenly, the fog opened up, surrounding him and in some way pulling him onto the glowing water. John frantically tried paddling his small boat away and off the strange water, but it was a useless effort. As he settled down, he began to see a medium-sized houseboat floating in front of him. *What is that doing out here especially at this time of night?* he thought.

He suddenly saw two people moving around the deck of the boat. It was as though there was a spot-light beaming down on the boat coming from some-where above. "Hey, over here. Hey, over here!" he yelled while waving his hands. The two people didn't hear him and seemed to be hurrying frantically about the deck of the boat. *What's going on? They should be able to hear me. I'm right here,* he thought.

John grabbed his paddles and started to try to row to the boat, but he couldn't get any closer to the boat than he already was. He stopped to rest when he heard the two arguing intensely. The man on the boat seemed to be furious about something. John could hear the two screaming at each other, but he couldn't make out what they were arguing about. *If I could just get a little closer,* he thought.

Suddenly, a gust of wind blew in from behind, and his small craft began drifting toward the large boat. As he approached within fifteen feet, he yelled out again, "Hey, I could use some help out here. Hey!

can you hear me up there?" For a second time, they didn't seem to notice. *That's impossible,* he thought.

The young woman began running toward the front of the boat as John could only observe. The man was yelling at her to stop and come back to the back of the boat, but she didn't. To John, it looked as though she didn't want to be near the guy.

Suddenly, the young woman from the front of the boat shouted back, saying, "Ken, I've got to. I can't take this anymore!"

The man in the back of the boat seemed to relax and calm himself down, speaking with a gentler tone in his voice. He said, "Now let's think this through. You can handle this. We all can. We just have to calm down and get ourselves together. If you tell anyone about this, especially the authorities, well, it will destroy us all. Don't you see that?"

She stood there, listening and trembling with fear. Ken began to move slowly toward her. She had her head down, not paying attention to Ken. It was as though she was thinking about what he had said and in some way trying to make some sense of their disagreement. She had become relaxed, but as Ken grew closer, her anxiety returned.

She said, "No. Stop." And she raised her hands. "I don't want you near me right now!"

"Now look, it's not that difficult to understand. If you go to the authorities, you'll ruin my career and my family's reputation. I can't allow you to do that. Don't you see?" he said with a new almost-possessed-like evil look on his face.

She screamed as she tried to move farther away from the guy, saying, "Just stay away and take me back to shore."

He began to move closer to her with a greater sense of urgency. As he got within arm's reach, he suddenly lunged toward her, grabbing her arm. She let out a loud scream, yelling for someone to help her as she pulled away. She then ran toward the rear of the boat, picking up a large wooden oar that was laying on the deck to protect herself as she made her way to the back of the boat. John stood up in his little boat, saying, "Hey, there. Over here. Jump in, and I'll get you!"

But she didn't seem to hear his offer for help. She stood at the rear of the boat, holding the oar out as if she was ready to strike Ken if he approached too close. She looked frantically for somewhere to go for safety. Her head turned as she was looking over the edge of the boat, her eyes focusing on the luminescent water.

John thought that for an instant, she looked directly at him, so he tried again, "Hey, I'm right here. Jump in, and I'll pick you up!" She turned around and was looking over the back of the boat as though she was getting ready to jump. Ken started running toward her, and as he got close, he lunged at her for a second time. He had this crazed look on his face that John recognized from his earlier dream when Ken was attacking Susan.

Before John could do anything to warn her, she wheeled around with the oar and struck Ken on the head. He grabbed his forehead and grimaced with pain, falling to the deck of the boat. The woman dropped the oar and reached down to help him up, saying that she was sorry, but he only became more violent.

He then pushed her back, and as she fell, he said angrily, "You shouldn't have done that. You shouldn't have done that at all." His forehead was bleeding profusely as he slowly stood up over her.

Without hesitation, he quickly reached down, picked her up, and threw her overboard. She began splashing about in the water, pleading for Ken to help pull her back onto the boat. He didn't say a word. He stared down at her with a cold, evil look.

Then he reached down and picked up the oar and held it up high over his head. He yelled, "I told you it would all work out, didn't I?" His face filled with rage as the girl became desperate to swim away. She screamed as the oar slammed down on her shoulder. The blow seemed to stun her, and she began to struggle just to stay afloat. Then the oar came down for a second time, striking her on the side of her head. As the blood began to fill the water around her, she began pleading with him to stop, but he didn't. He raised the oar for a third and final time and struck a blow that silenced her cries. She became very still in the water as Ken seemed to be satisfied that she was dead. He threw the oar down and pulled her body next to the boat. Her body was floating just under the surface of the water, not moving, just bouncing up and down with the waves.

"Why won't you sink?" Ken said in a frustrated tone. He then looked around the boat and retrieved a rope tied onto an anchor. "This should do," he said. Ken took the rope and tied it off firmly to the woman's legs and then dropped the anchor. She seemed to simply disappear in the darkness of the water.

John was stunned as he witnessed the entire event. He became angry to think that this guy Ken had killed for a second time and that there was nothing that he could do to help. He grabbed at his chest, looking for his gun, but he wasn't wearing it. Just then, he heard the engines on the boat start up.

John sat back and watched as it slipped away into the darkness. He lay back in his boat extremely exhausted and frustrated. He closed his eyes and felt the relaxing waves underneath him.

Suddenly, he heard, "John. John. John!" He opened his eyes to see Dex standing over him.

"What are you doing here?" asked John.

"What? What am I doing here? Remember we came here last night," replied Dex.

"We did. What? I was on the water. How did I get back in this room?" asked a confused John.

"Man, you must have had some kind of dream."

"Huh? What? A dream. More like a vision. That was no dream!"

CHAPTER 18

The storm had passed, and the two men awoke to an unusually bright sunny day. The rays from the sun were beginning to filter in through the window of their room, creating an illuminating effect and adding much-needed warmth that both men desired.

Dex, however, was still extremely cold and kept complaining that he just couldn't seem to shake his deep-felt chill. He wrapped himself with the blanket from his bed as he moved around the room. First, building a roaring fire from the logs that were left-over from the night before. Then he brewed his usual pot of coffee in which to start the day.

John lay in bed as he told Dex all about his dream. Dex seemed to be listening to every word and every detail, not wanting to miss anything about John's new dream. Neither man knew what to think of John's dream. It just didn't seem to fit with the dream that he had back in Boston about the art student from Harvard.

Somewhat confused, John got out of his bed and made his way over to the window as Dex handed him a cup of coffee. He looked out and saw that it was extremely bright outside. "Not a cloud in the sky," he said as he squinted. The sun was reflecting off the snow, creating an intense glare that was very painful to his eyes. The glare was so intense that he could barely stand to look at it as he turned away and began rubbing his eyes.

He said, "Dex, I hope you brought some sunglasses. You're gonna need 'em today!"

"I just hope that it warms up out there," responded Dex.

John turned back to look out of the window for a second time, allowing his eyes time to adjust to the bright glare from the snow. This time, he took a longer and slower look, almost as if he were looking specifically for something. *What is that?* he thought. He began wiping the fog away from the window to get a clearer look.

"Steam," he said softly.

"What? What did you say?" asked Dex.

John didn't respond as he continued wiping away the fog from the window, taking an even more intense look. He went to the door, jerked it open, and stood there, looking out in front of the cabin. About one hundred or so yards in front of their room was the lake with steam rising off the water just as he had seen it in his dream. Dex soon made his way over to the door and stood there alongside John. John looked at Dex with a weird look on his face.

"This is just as I saw it in my dream. The lake, the boat on the shore, and the well. Right there in the middle of the grounds. It's all here," he muttered.

John turned to go back inside, leaving Dex at the door still wrapped up in his blanket.

He immediately began hurrying to put on his clothes as Dex said, "Well, wait for me," as he, too, scrambled to get dressed. The two men started out the door as John noticed a set of tracks in the snow. He made a foot impression next to one of the tracks to compare. They matched perfectly.

"I don't believe this," John said as he looked over at Dex. They followed the tracks out to the lake's edge. It was exactly as it had occurred in his dream.

"This is too weird. Don't tell me that I was actually out there on this lake last night. That was just a dream. Wasn't that just a dream?" he asked Dex with a confused look on his face. However, Dex couldn't offer John any reassuring or a comforting explanation as to what he seemed to be experiencing.

"You didn't wake up in the middle of the night and notice that I was missing from my bed last night, did you?" asked John.

"No. No. Once I fell asleep, I didn't wake up until morning," replied Dex.

John turned and looked toward the middle of the lake. He took a deep breath and whispered just under his breath, "There must be someone out there then."

"What? What did you say?" asked Dex.

While holding a deep penetrating stare toward the middle of the lake, John walked closer to the water's edge and repeated himself. Dex had never seen such a strange look on his friend's face before.

They had been through many tough and difficult times together, and in all his years of knowing John, he had never seen a look on his face like this one before. It was intense and troublesome to Dex seeing his friend this way.

Dex grabbed John by the arm and gently shook him while saying, "John. John, what did you say about someone being out there?"

"That's right. That's right. There must be someone out there in this lake. A body and no one knows that she's out there. I had that dream for a reason. The body of a young woman is in this lake. I guarantee it, and it's not Susan. No, it's not Susan. It's someone else."

John turned and looked at Dex with this frightened look. Dex always believed that John was strong and virtually never feared anything, but in some way, this was different.

Dex began to get an uneasy feeling as John continued, "I have a real bad feeling about all this. This guy Ken, he's pure evil. He killed this girl on his boat and then left her. He's the only one that knows she's out there in this water. He's evil. I saw it in his face both times when I had those dreams on the boat and at the art studio. It's like he gets this evil, uncontrollable, and distorted look on his face, pure evil, almost like he's possessed by an evil spirit."

"What? Man, stop it. You're getting nuts."

"Think about it. Just stop and think about it. All this strange stuff going on around us. There is more to this Ken fellow than we realize."

"Like what? Like he's a devil or a demon or something. Yeah, right!" said Dex as he chuckled and then took a big gulp.

"Hey, I'm not saying that, but just try to explain some of the things that have been happening to both of us. You can't, can you?" John asked.

"No, I can't," replied Dex.

"Okay. I'm just saying that there seem to be some evil forces around this guy Ken. That's all. Something that we've never seen before," said John.

Dex started to laugh and then began to look concerned as he, too, turned to look toward the deep water of the lake.

Dex took another big gulp and asked softly, "Yeah, but how can you be so sure that there is a woman's body out there?"

"Like I said, I had that dream for a reason. Someone or something is trying to tell me something." John turned to look around at the ground as he followed the path of the tracks in the snow. He pointed down, saying, "Look at these tracks and that little boat over there. I was in that boat, and I was on this lake last night. Everything that I saw in my dream actually happened."

"That's impossible," said Dex as he shook his head in disbelief.

"I know it sounds impossible, but has anything made sense lately? Why are we even here? No, it's very possible all right. We're here for a reason and that girl that's out in this water, she's a part of this whole thing." Dex seemed to reluctantly agree as they both moved over to the tiny boat. As they walked up, Dex noticed something in the boat that seemed to be out of place.

He reached down, picked up the object, and said, "Well, someone's been in this boat." He was holding in his hand a yellow flashlight that was still shining.

John's eyes grew wide as he noticed it and said, "That's mine. I had it with me last night." Dex threw the flashlight down and jumped away from the boat as if he were afraid of it.

"Then you really were out there last night," he cried. John could only shake his head as he, too, found it all too hard to believe.

Suddenly, a deep-sounding voice was heard by both men that seemed to echo through the resort. They turned, looked back toward their cabin, and saw a large man running toward them, waving his hands. At first, they thought it was that crazy guy Rick from the restaurant. But as he got closer, they realized that they had no idea who this person was or even where he came from. He seemed to be concerned about something. "Hey, are you two crazy? What are you doing out there?" he shouted. John and Dex moved nervously away from the boat, almost as though they were guilty of doing something wrong, but they weren't sure of what.

Suddenly, they began hearing several loud popping and cracking noises that seemed to be coming from below their feet. They stopped and looked at each other with a worried look on their face.

Confused as to what the noises were, they just stood there as if they were waiting for what might happen next. Then more whining and loud cracking noises vibrated across the lake.

At exactly the same time, both realized that they were standing on a thin layer of ice. The snow from last night had covered the lake's edge, and neither of them realized that they were about twenty yards from the bank. Dex, frozen with fear, managed to softly irk out the words, "Oh shit," as he stood there staring at John. They could see that the water was beginning to bubble up through the cracks as the ice was becoming more unstable.

The large man who had seemed to have appeared out of nowhere stopped at the bank's edge and said, "That ice isn't thick enough for ice fishing yet. Just stay put. Don't move a muscle. I'll go get a rope."

John yelled back at the man, "Well, could ya hurry up? I'm not sure how long this is going to hold."

The man waved back and hurried off. As soon as he got out of sight, another loud pop, then another and another. The water was bubbling up from out of the cracks even more than ever.

John looked over at Dex and said, "I don't think he's going to make it back in time." Standing as still as possible, Dex looked back at John.

"Hey, John," Dex shouted as he began to laugh. "Did I ever tell you that I don't know how to swim?"

"What? You don't know how to swim. Hell, everyone knows how to swim," replied John as he, too, laughed in disbelief.

"No, seriously, I never learned."

"Well, I wouldn't worry about it if I were you. Hell! If you fall in there, you'll probably freeze to death before you drown," John said as he chuckled.

"Yeah, I guess so," responded Dex as a half-nervous smile began to appear on his face.

Both men began to slowly slide their feet on the ice, moving ever so slowly toward the bank. With every movement, the ice cracked louder and was becoming more unstable. Then suddenly, the ice gave way.

Dex disappeared under the surface of the water as John dove toward the small boat, landing in the small craft. He rolled around and started screaming for Dex, but Dex wasn't anywhere in sight. He grabbed the flashlight in the boat and began shining it down into the darkness of the cold water, but still, no Dex. John kept screaming his name, but there was nothing, not even air bubbles. The water was like ice. It was extremely cold, and he knew that he had a very short amount of time to get Dex out of that water.

He stood up in the tiny boat and jumped in after his friend. The water was colder than he had even imagined. As he hit the water, his body seemed to go into instant shock. A tingling sensation and the feeling of thousands of tiny needles began to run through his entire body. His arms and legs began to cramp from the intense cold, making it impossible to move. His chest began to burn with pain from the lack of air, then his body began to relax as he went numb.

Floating still and motionless in the water, he began seeing images of his wife. Oh, how beautiful she was, her smile, her sparkling blue eyes. How he missed her so. He seemed to be at ease with what was happening, and he knew that it wouldn't be long before it would all be over. If there was a possibility that by dying he could be with his wife, then he was ready, he thought. So he relaxed and began to accept his fate.

Suddenly, a jerk, then he felt a strange squeezing feeling around his wrist as he was hurled upward toward the surface. As his body rose up to the surface, he took a big deep breath of air. His eyes began to clear as he looked up toward the brightness of the sun. Seeing a silhouette, John could only make out the image of a woman standing over him. "Angelica?" he asked softly. However, she didn't respond. Exhausted, John closed his eyes and blacked out.

CHAPTER 19

John slipped in and out of consciousness for the next several hours. He had been taken to a darkened room that seemed to have an old, stale, musty odor that hung heavily throughout the room. His breathing was shallow as he lay motionless in the deep pillows of the bed. Lingering on the edge of death, John's body was in a coma-type state, struggling internally to survive. To John, it was as though he were in some sort of deep hole, looking up and having no strength to pull himself out. He thought to himself how easy it would be to just relax, take one last breath, and then not breathe anymore. John was tired, and he was ready, so he took one last breath and then relaxed.

In his mind, he began seeing sparks or flashes of light that were dancing and swirling all around him. He tried to reach out and touch one, but his hands weren't fast enough. *That's strange*, he thought to himself as he tried to figure out what these tiny sparks of light might be.

Then slowly, a soft image of two people began to appear in front of him. The sparks of light began to fade away as he realized that it was Dex and Angelica.

They seemed to be waving at him, motioning for him to come over. John smiled and yelled out, "Hey, Dex, I thought you were dead."

But Dex didn't respond with an answer. He just smiled back and continued to motion for him to come over. As he looked closer, he realized that they were standing in front of the old well, which was located in the center of the resort. "So, guys, what is it?"

To John, they both looked kind of strange. They had this weird transparent look, and other than the one smile from Dex, they both seemed to be showing no signs of emotion. *This is strange*, John thought. *Okay, I get it. I'm having one of these weird dreams. I'll just go with it.*

The two kept waving for John to come over with what looked like an almost-desperate plea for him to come see something. Dex and Angelica turned away from John as they both began looking down the well followed by intense waving as if they needed John to come quick. "Okay. Okay. I'm coming!"

John hurried over, and as he got to within fifteen feet of the well, the two stopped waving and began pointing at something high up on the hill. John stopped and looked in the direction of their point. They were pointing upward toward the peak of a nearby mountaintop that overlooked the resort and the valley floor.

High up on the mountaintop was a huge mansion of a home that seemed out of place among its rustic surroundings. *What a beautiful home*, he thought.

But who would live way out here in the middle of who knows where? He then realized that they were trying to tell him something. But what?

He turned his sights back to Dex and Angelica to try to get some sort of explanation as to what's up with this giant house. What's so important about it that they had to point it out? To his surprise, they were both gone, no trace, no nothing, except that old well.

John began shouting, "Hey, guys, what is it? Dex, Angelica, where did you go. What is it? Angelica!"

Then out of nowhere, John felt a slap on his face, then another and another. Then he began hearing a strange and unfamiliar voice, saying, "No. There's no Angelica here. It's just me."

John opened his eyes to find that he was in this big soft bed with quilted blankets piled so high on top of him that he couldn't move if he wanted to. His eyes were weak, but the vision of an old man began to appear in front of him.

"Who are you?" asked John.

"My English name is Charlie or Charles as my friends call me. My Indian name is White Feather. I'm a full-blooded Native American Indian." John lay in bed staring at the old man, not knowing where he was or how long he had been there. He looked around the room, observing the old Indian artifacts as the old man continued, "Yeah, it's a funny thing, you know."

"What's that?" asked John.

"The way we Indians get our names. In the old days, we didn't pass our names down like your White culture does." The old man paused as he looked up and around the room. "To give you an idea on how it works, a friend of mine, fellow tribesmen, went by the name of Duke after the great John Wayne. He always liked his movies, well, most of them. Anyway, he took that name because his Indian name was Squatting Dog. He didn't like that name too much," the old Indian said as he chuckled.

"So your Indian name is White Feather?" asked John.

"Yeah, that's right. Seems that when I was born, my mother saw a flock of white birds flying around. They look sort of like a blue jay but they're not. They are white with blue-jay markings. Some say that they have mystical qualities and that they come around only when we are in need of help. They come around to offer guidance to those that need it most."

John sat up quickly and said with some excitement, "Really? You're kidding. White birds, a flock of them. I've recently had some encounters with the most unusual kind of blue jay myself, very interesting birds."

The old man smiled and said, "Yeah, highly intelligent birds, you know."

"Well, they helped me get through some difficult times," replied John. John smiled and then raised his head up to look around the room. "Where's Dex?" he asked.

"Dex. Is that the name of the guy that you were with? Sorry, but when I came back, you were on the shore of the lake. There was no sign of your friend. You started mumbling something, but I couldn't make it out." John lay his head back down on the thick pillow and then put his hands on his face. He became very quiet as he replayed the events of that morning in his mind. Then the old man elaborated with a soft and saddened voice, "I'm deeply sorry. I looked, but there was nothing. No sign of him anywhere. I knew that I had to get you inside and warmed up before hypothermia set in, so I brought you in here. I went back to see if I could locate your friend, but still, there was nothing. I'll get the authorities out here on Monday when the roads become passable. Until then, just try to relax and try to get your strength back."

The old Indian got up and began moving around the room almost as if he was trying to avoid eye contact with John. He felt guilty because he was unable to get to Dex, so he suddenly seemed to make himself extremely busy. There was an uneasy quiet that began to fill the room. Neither John nor the old Indian seemed to have anything else to talk about. As he left the room, he turned and said to John, "Now you just lie there and relax. I'll get you some warm broth to help take the chill out."

John didn't respond. Instead, he just lay there, looking out the window as the sun began to fall behind the mountaintop. A dark shadow moved slowly across the valley floor as it looked like another very dark and cold night was on the way.

It wasn't long before the old man came back into the room, carrying a tray. On it was a large bowl with steam rising up into the cold air of the room.

"I hope you like chicken soup. You know, this is the best stuff ever made for taking out a chill or getting over a sickness." John sat up in bed. He hadn't eaten anything all day and was quite hungry. The old man looked at John and smiled, saying, "This is an old family recipe. I've been making this stuff for as long as I can remember. Basically, it's egg noodles with a thickened broth and large chunks of chicken. This will warm up your bones and keep pneumonia from setting in."

"Sounds great!" replied John.

John could feel the warmth of the soup traveling throughout his body with every spoonful that he swallowed, and it wasn't long before he began regaining his strength. The old man stood and watched with delight as John engulfed the bowl of soup. By now, the sun had completely gone down behind the mountaintop, and the valley was a pitch-black dark, an incredible black dark like the previous night.

John asked, "Does it always get this dark around here?"

The old man looked at John with a strange and concerned look on his face. "Yeah. It's been like this for years," he said as he turned to look out the window.

"For years!" John repeated. "What does that mean—for years?"

The old man continued to gaze out the window with a bit of a disturbed look on his face. He stood in the middle of the room, not saying a word, simply looking out the window. After a few quiet moments, he began to speak with a new tone, a concerned tone in his voice as John listened to every word.

"Ever since they took down the signs to this place and disconnected the phones out here, it's like this place died or simply stopped to exist."

Charles turned away from the window and moved over to the fireplace where he began building a fire for the evening. John sat in bed and watched as Charles carefully stacked the wood in the fireplace and then started the fire. He waited quietly as Charles finished with the fire. It was almost as if he seemed reluctant to continue with his explanation and in some way wanted to choose his words carefully, for he knew that his story would not be easy to believe.

Then he turned to John, took a deep breath, and said, "It all started about fifteen years ago after the old owners sold out. This place has never been the same. Funny thing though. The new owners never did a thing with this place. It's as though they simply bought it and then just closed it up. Seemed like something evil settled in around this place."

Charles paused and went over to the window for another look outside before he continued. John could tell that he seemed very uncomfortable, so he patiently waited for Charles to continue, not wanting to interrupt or distract from his train of thought. He turned and looked at John, then down at the floor. After what seemed to be a couple of intense minutes, he looked back up at John with a distressed and almost-paranoid look as he started again.

"Yeah, I took care of the horses at the stable barn back in those days. Part of my job was to take the tourists out for rides in the mountains. Those were good times back then. In some way, it reminded me of being with my tribal ancestors. The thought of riding in these mountains on some of the same trails that were carved out and used by my ancestors. Well, I don't expect you to understand how that makes me feel. But it was like going back in time, almost like riding alongside them as we meandered our way through the mountains. Unfortunately, that all changed when the Daultry family bought this place and then just closed it off."

"Who? Who did you say bought this place?" asked John as he perked up to hear more.

"The Daultrys, a big wealthy family. Legal crooks. That's what I call them. Your people call 'em lawyers. They own a big law firm and play politics for fun. They simply ruin people's lives and then walk away, heading straight to the bank," he replied.

"It sounds like you know these people pretty well," said John.

"Yeah. Even though I hate what they did to this place, they still sign my check. You see, I was hired by the family's son, Kenneth. He came out one day as I was cleaning out the stalls and asked me if I would be interested in staying on and overseeing the place. Since I loved it out here so much, I couldn't refuse, especially since he offered to pay me about fifty thousand a year and that I had to live out here. A week later, he just showed up and said that no one could come here anymore and that I was to make sure of it. He said that this place is closed until further notice by him only. That was fifteen years ago. Eventually, he would build a big house up on the ridge above this place. He lives up there now. I guess he wants to make sure I'm doing my job."

John got up from the bed and made his way over to the window as well. He stood there, looking and thinking about the story that he had just been told. He turned to look back at Charles and noticed that he had a new disturbing look on his face.

"That's not the strangest part to this story. Let me ask you something before we continue," asked Charles.

"Yeah. Okay. What?" replied John.

"This is going to sound like I'm just a crazy Indian, but I have to ask you this. Do you believe that there is something out there or someplace that we go—you know, our spirits—after our bodies die?"

"Charles, if you had asked me that two years ago, I would have said that I just wasn't sure, like everybody you listen to, the religious fanatics, and the hardcore churchgoers and their preaching. Then something happens in your life, and you just don't know what to believe. You're just empty inside. So to answer your question, two years ago, I would have said NO. But after what I've been through the last week or so, I would have to say that I definitely believe that there is something out there, someplace that our souls go," John said with a grin.

Charles looked reassured that he could now continue with his story.

"Would you believe then that a person's soul could also get caught somewhere in a limbo or refuse to go to wherever we're supposed to go to?" asked Charles.

"I suppose so," replied a troubled John.

"So if you believe that we do have a soul that is supposed to go somewhere, would you then believe that some of those souls can become angry, refusing to leave, becoming an evil, haunting spirit or ghost?"

John replied, "I suppose so," as he frowned.

Charles hurried over to where John was standing near the window. He reached out and grabbed him by both arms and with a trembling voice, said, "There's something evil out there. Some evil spirit walks these grounds. I think it's a woman. Occasionally, I can hear her screaming at night, terrible, desperate screams. I think that Kenneth Daultry killed someone, hid her body out there somewhere, and then bought this place so she would never be found."

Extremely nervous, Charles turned away and hurried back over to the fire. It all seemed to make sense to John. *That's why I'm here. Susan Ashworth's body must be out here. But where?* he wondered.

"I've seen things around here too. I've seen lights come on down at the old lodge. There is no one here but me. Thinking that Mr. Daultry may be down there, I'll go down to the lodge and check it out, but when I get down there, nothing. The lights go off. Nothing. No one. And then I'll hear soft giggling or laughing, you know, like someone just played a prank. I just ignore stuff now. I don't even go outside around here at night anymore."

"Yeah, I imagine so," replied John. "Say, is there an old couple running the restaurant at the entrance to this place?" asked John.

"No. That's actually the lodge. But, no, there is no one running the place. It closed fifteen years ago with the rest of this place. Why? Have you seen something too?" Charles asked.

"Uh, yeah," replied John as he pulled back the curtains to take a look over at the restaurant.

John stood at the window and stared out at the darkness. Again, it was pitch black outside. There was no moonlight or stars in the night sky to help ease the darkness, just darkness. It made John sad to think that his friend was out there somewhere in the water.

New anger began to boil inside John as he realized that in some way, Ken Daultry was now the cause of his friend's death, another victim of this man's evil. And he realized more than ever that he must see this thing through by bringing Ken to justice. *It's time that I have a talk with this Ken*, he thought. *In the morning, I'm going to go up there. I'm going to go up to his house. Somehow I'm going to meet this guy face-*

to-face. With that thought, John turned around. The old man was gone. He was alone.

The flickering flames from the fireplace gave the room a soft, soothing feeling as John went over to a nearby chair and sat down. He wanted to wait for the old man to return so that he could ask more questions about Kenneth, but he didn't. John sat in the chair and stared at the flames. The fire softly cracked and popped, which had a strange calming and relaxing effect. And it wasn't long before John had fallen to sleep.

CHAPTER 20

John was awoken out of a hard sleep by some faint out-of-place noise. "Where am I?" he asked himself as he sat up in the chair. The fire was out, and the room was dark. It seemed to be unexplainably cold in the room. It reminded him of the incident inside his car after he did away with Nick and Telly at Mystic Lake. A deep penetrating chill surged through his body, and his breath began to freeze as it hit the icy cold air. The only light in the room was the soft glow of the embers coming from the fireplace. Somewhat disoriented, he noticed an old half-burned candle on the table next to him. He grabbed it and then went over to the fireplace. *Maybe I can get this thing lit*, he thought to himself.

He began stoking up the fire to get a flame so that he could light the candle. John began blowing on the embers as he continued to stoke. Finally, a flame. The warmth was immediate as the heat from the fire cut through the icy air. He stuck the small wick from the candle as close to the fire as possible, and it took. Now with a small amount of light, John could see through the darkness of the room. *Maybe a window blew open*, he thought.

As he quietly moved around the room, he never realized just how big the room was until now. His breath, frozen in the air as he breathed, seemed to give John an uncomfortable and uneasy feeling. As John moved about, the candle would light up small portions of the room, allowing John to see the many small figurines that the old man, Charles, had accumulated throughout the years. The flickering flame from the candle seemed to make the figurines come to life, their tiny eyes fixed on John's every movement and their shadows bouncing and moving in some methodical evil dance.

The strange room began to tear down John's ability to think rationally as he was wanting to find some comfort in his surroundings, but he couldn't. The room seemed to grow colder and colder as he moved farther away from the fireplace. He slowly made his way around the room, checking all the windows, but none were open. *Man, it's cold, too cold*, he thought.

He noticed an old handmade quilt draped over the end of the bed. He picked it up and quickly wrapped it around himself. The thick quilt was soothing for an instant but then the quilt turned to an icy cold, making him feel even colder than he already was. *What is going on? It shouldn't be this cold in here. I just need to get that fire going again*, he thought. He remembered seeing a rather large stack of firewood next to the fireplace.

He turned and raised his candle to see his way back across the large room. As he looked up, he could see the silhouette of what looked like a young woman sitting in the chair that he had been sleeping in.

"Who are you?" he asked. She didn't say a word. She then rose up and began moving slowly toward John. He held out the candle as she approached in the hopes that he could get a better look. An eerie feeling surged through John as she had this strange, frightening look about her.

"Who are you? Can I help you with something?" John asked again, only now with a nervous and shaken voice. Again, she had no reply as she continued to move closer and closer toward John. With his eyes open wide, all he could do was stand there and wait while holding out the candle.

He began seeing her image more clearly as she got closer. He could see that she had long, thick dark-brown hair and that she seemed to be moving in some weird gliding manner as she came nearer and nearer. Once she came within five feet of John, he was able to gather enough of his senses to motion her to stop. He held his hand up, and to his surprise, she did.

"Okay. That's close enough. Now who are you?" John asked again. He waited, but again, she offered no response. Already nervous, John began to offer some rational explanation as to why he was there. "Well, I'm John. I'm just spending the night. I'll be leaving in the morning. Do you live here with the old man?" John suddenly realized, *No. She doesn't live out here with the old man. He said he lives out here by himself.*

An eerie feeling began to surge through him as the young woman just stood there staring, not saying a word. Suddenly, an unearthly foul odor, like the smell of death, began to resonate throughout the room. John's throat began to tighten and close up as he tried to breathe in the cold air in the room. He grasped his throat and fell back onto the floor. He clutched the candle and somehow managed to hold it up as he lay on his back while trying to breathe.

With a gliding motion, the woman quickly moved over to John and seemed to hover above him. She looked down at him as he lay there. The stench was horrific. Unable to move or speak, John lay there and looked up at the strange woman, wondering to himself what might happen next.

Suddenly, the woman's face became angry as she floated down to with in inches of his face. "Why are you here? No one comes to this place!" she said with an evil tone. John's body seemed to be paralyzed with fear as he lay there, looking up at the woman. As she spoke, the tightening in John's throat seemed to be relaxing, allowing him to catch his breath. "I ask again. Why are you here?" she asked with the same angry tone.

Unable to speak because of the choking odor, he realized that this woman was the same woman on the boat. The woman he saw in his dream with Kenneth Daultry. He realized while exchanging heavy eye contact with the woman that she was supposed to be dead.

His heart was racing, and somehow, he managed to softly eke out the words, "I'm here to help."

"Help. How can you help? You can't help!" she responded.

"Justice. I'll get justice for you. That's how I will help," he responded softly.

As he spoke those words, the foul odor began to subside, allowing John to breathe more normally. The woman began to raise back away from John, which gave him the opportunity to sit up in a more comfortable position.

"He'll never get justice, not until he's dead!" she remarked.

"If anyone deserves to be killed for what they've done in their life, it's him. But I'm here to see him go to jail. I'm not here to kill him," replied John.

With that, the woman became angry for a second time and swooped back over John, forcing him to lie back on the floor. The foul odor began to return, causing him to choke. He could feel the tightening in his throat returning for a second time, making him weak as he struggled to breathe.

She was within inches of his face, allowing him to see the ravages of death. Her appearance changed almost instantly. Instead of the previously dark, beautiful, bouncy hair and soft skin, it was now matty and stringy with bald patches on her torn scalp. The flesh from her face became dry and prune-like as if the radiant energy of life had been sucked out of it. Some of the skin dangled from her cheek and was close to falling off. Pale and black areas covered the remaining areas of flesh as a greenish-colored slim oozed out and down the side of her head from the gaping wound of the oar. Her eyes were now drawn and sunken into the sockets of her skull. He was shocked and disgusted by her new appearance as he continued to struggle on the floor.

He tried desperately to get up, but his body was weak. It was as though he was paralyzed and didn't have the strength to resist. He could feel a new tightening in his chest as his heart struggled to beat and the life in his body began to fade. With an angry tone, the ghostly woman spoke again, "Now you leave this place. I'll take care of Daultry my way!"

John lay there, waiting. His heart struggled with each beat, and his body grew weaker and weaker. *Dying is easy*, he thought to himself. As John began to fade in and out of consciousness, he began repeating, *This is easy. This is easy. It's easy*, as he closed his eyes for the last time.

Suddenly, a bright light began to appear. The light grew brighter and brighter, filling the room with each passing moment. The image of another young woman began to appear. She seemed soothing, and the familiar fragrance of jasmine began to emerge. The foul odor was almost immediately forgotten as John's senses concentrated on the new refreshing aroma. His body was becoming stronger as the other woman was getting closer, and he began to recognize her face.

"John. John, you must get up now," she said in a soft tone. He had forgotten a long time ago what his wife's voice sounded like, but in an instant, when she spoke, the memory of her delicate voice came back. A surge of emotion raced through his soul, and he tried desperately to get up, but he was still too weak. His wife reached out and offered her hand.

"Eve, is it really you?" John asked.

"Yes, it's really me. Now take my hand."

John reached up, and she took his hand. Sparks of energy began to flood through his body, making him stronger as she helped him to his feet. She looked exactly as she had at the football game that day two years ago, the last time he saw her. She smiled at him, and immediately, tears began to fall down his cheeks. He couldn't speak as he was overcome with emotion. All he could do was hold her in a tight embrace, never wanting to let go. It was a warm and soothing feeling, a feeling that he thought he would never feel again. She as well didn't want to let go, and the memories of their love for one another proved as strong now as it ever had. They stood there, taking their time, enjoying the moment.

In a gentle tone, she softly said, "You must go on. You still have things that you must do."

"What? I don't want to go on, not without you," John replied as he shook his head.

"But you must. It's not you're time yet. You still have things you must do. Helping people with their problems, that's what you must do. And even though I would rather have you here with me, I also know that your life isn't finished. You must understand that there is a reason for you to go forward with your life. It's not complete," she said as she pushed away.

John grabbed Eve and pulled her tight against him. He closed his eyes and felt his wife's body against his, and then suddenly, she was gone. John, still holding an embrace, opened his eyes and looked around. The room was empty. He was alone, and it was becoming dark again. He was sad by his wife's sudden disappearance, but he also felt a newfound sense of energy.

Then a familiar panic began to set in. The icy cold air from the room hit John like a ton of bricks. *I've got to get that fire going*, he thought. He quickly went to the stack of wood and began building a roaring fire in the fireplace. Then he lit every candle in the room that he could find. Nervous that the angry ghost might return, he sat up the rest of the night— sitting in the chair next to to the fire wide awake with the room as bright as possible.

CHAPTER 21

The next morning, John woke, still sitting in the chair he had collapsed in. After all he had experienced, he had somehow fallen into a deep sound sleep. His body was exhausted from the weird unexplainable events of the previous night and the long trip that brought him to this place. He seemed to be in no hurry to wake, for it was the first sound sleep that he had had in a very long time.

Suddenly, a pop and a slow creaking noise penetrated the peaceful silence of the room. John's eyes snapped open as he seemed to look quickly around the room. Nervous about his unfamiliar surroundings and the events from the night before. His mind began to race, *What the hell am I doing? I got to get out of here. I don't want that thing coming back.* With that, John grabbed his clothes, got dressed, and quickly left the room.

As he made his way through the house, trying to find his way to the outside, he realized that it didn't seem as though this place had been inhabited for many years. The rooms were dark, dusty, and filled with cobwebs. The floor was covered with dirt, leaves, and what looked like small rodent droppings.

It just smelled old and empty. *What happened to the old man?* he thought. "Hey, is anybody here?" he shouted. But there was no response. The whole place just made John feel even more uneasy than he already was. He whirled around and saw an old wooden door. *Hopefully, that's the way out of here,* he thought.

As he approached the door, he noticed what looked like a huge spiderweb that hung down from the ceiling to about halfway down to the middle of the door. Inside the web was a ginormous spider. It looked as though it was ready to pounce on anything that unknowingly touched the web. *Geez, that thing is huge. That must be some hairy giant mountain wood spider or something*, he thought. John turned, leaving the spider behind, and it wasn't long before he finally found himself exiting the house through another door.

Outside the ground was covered with bright white snow, and above the sky was billowing with dark purple fast-moving clouds. It looked as though any moment it could begin snowing again. The cold air shot quickly through John's body as a deep penetrating chill began to settle in. "What time of the day is it?" he asked himself. He looked down at his watch. It read 3:27 a.m. "That can't be right!" He tapped on the watch and looked again, then he noticed that the second hand wasn't working. That time kept going through his head: 3:27 a.m. Then it dawned on him. That was the exact time that his wife and children had died. A deep, sad emotion filled his heart as he reached down to unsnap the watch, then he snapped it back. It was his wedding gift. He had it all these years and never had a problem with it. *I'll see if I can get someone to fix it later*, he thought.

John raised his head to look over his surroundings. He noticed that in the middle of the resort was a well, much like the one that he envisioned in his dream from the night before. He trudged through the deep snow to get a closer look and hung his head over the edge to look down the shaft. He could only see about five feet before the darkness overtook his ability to see any farther. Suddenly, a cold burst of wind blew up from the shaft, forcing John to turn and look away. He leaned back on the brick wall that surrounded the shaft. Blinking a few times, he was able to refocus his vision as he noticed a huge mansion of a home that sat up on the ridge. It seemed to be in the perfect location to overlook the entire valley. As he looked around the rest of the ridges surrounding the valley, he realized that this was the only house anywhere to be seen. *That must be it. That's where Daultry lives, the same one the old man was talking about*, he thought.

In a distance, John could hear in a soft familiar voice. Someone was calling his name, "John. John, come over here." He looked around to focus on the voice. It was Angelica. "Where have you been?" she asked.

"I was over here. I spent the night in that place," he said as he pointed toward the lodge.

"Well, we worried about you. We couldn't find you anywhere. We looked all over."

"We. We. What do you mean we?" asked John.

"You know, Dex," she said.

"Dex. You mean he's with you? I thought he drowned!"

"He would have if I hadn't gotten him out of that lake! We thought that you had died."

"Died. No, well, I guess I almost did," responded John. "If it wasn't for that old Indian pulling me out when he did, I probably would have."

"Old Indian. What old Indian? We are out here by ourselves," she said. "There's no one else out here but us, except for those old horses over there."

John looked around to see the horses. They were standing in a pen next to an old busted-up barn. It looked as though it definitely had seen better days. There were two horses. They just stood there, looking at John and Angelica. They had a strange expression on their faces, looking as though they hadn't seen any kind of excitement in a long time, much less any people to speak of. John thought, *There is something really strange about this place. Maybe Dex was right after all. Maybe this place does have ghosts or spirits or something.*

Suddenly, John's train of thought was interrupted by Angelica. "Hey, let's get out of the cold," she shouted. John trudged his way over to Angelica's cabin in the knee-deep snow. It seemed like a frozen tundra. Everything was white with thick mounds of snow covering everything as far as you could see.

As John reached the cabin, Angelica gave him a tight hug and then smiled. She then opened the door, and lying in bed under a deep layer of quilts was Dex. As the two men saw one another, a huge smile emerged over Dex's face.

In a weak voice, Dex said, "Man, I thought you were a goner!"

"I thought we were both goners," replied John as everyone began to laugh with relief.

"So where have you been?" asked Dex.

"I was on the other side of the resort. An old man, an Indian man who keeps care of this place, pulled me out of the water. He took me into a house. I guess it was connected to the old lodge. He warmed me up and gave me some soup. He had some strange things to say about this place. Funny thing though. I fell asleep after we talked for a while, and man, what a dream I had. This woman. I mean a creepy woman." About then, John could see that Dex was sitting up in bed, listening to every word. He felt as though if he continued with his story that Dex was going to start freaking out. "Well, it doesn't matter."

"What? What do you mean it doesn't matter? It matters. Now what happened?" asked Dex.

"No, really it wasn't that big of a deal. By the way, have either of you seen that old guy? He wasn't anywhere to be found this morning. It's like he just disappeared, and that house, it's like nobody has lived in it for years."

Dex suddenly jumped out of bed and said, "That's it. Let's just go. Let's just pack our shit and go. Let's get our stuff and leave now. There's too much weird stuff going on around here."

"No. We can't do that. The snow is too deep to try to drive out of here. I'm afraid we're just stuck here until either some of this snow melts or someone clears the road. Besides, I think I know where we can find Kenneth Daultry."

"You do? Really. Where?" asked Dex.

"Up on the ridge. I think he lives in that huge mansion on the ridge that overlooks this resort. According to the old Indian that runs this place, he bought the entire resort and then built that house on the ridge. I guess he wanted to keep a close eye on this place. What's weird about the whole thing is that he then hired the old man to oversee everything out here and then he told him to close this place up. He gave him specific instructions that absolutely no one was allowed to be here."

"Well, I still think that we need to just leave this place. This place is evil. Evil," said Dex.

Angelica reached over and touched Dex on the arm and with a soothing voice, said, "I think this is where we are supposed to be, Dex. We'll be fine. Even with all these strange events that seem to be happening to us all, we'll be fine as long as we believe in our faith."

"It's obvious that Daultry is hiding something out here, like a body," said John. "She's right. We're supposed to be here."

Dex turned and looked at John. He then turned away and started mumbling something to himself. At the same time, he began to let out a nervous laugh.

Neither John nor Angelica could quite make out what he was saying.

John interrupted the odd moment by saying, "Hey, what we have to do is to find a way up to the top of that ridge. We need to get to that mansion."

"What about the horses?" shouted Angelica. Both men looked at Angelica as she repeated, "The horses. They can get you up on that ridge!"

An anxious and excited look came over John's face. "Yeah. You're right! Lets' go see if we can find some saddles," replied John.

The three headed out the door of the cabin and began to make their way over to the stables. Angelica and John could hear Dex mumbling again to himself in a soft tone.

"Great! Horses! Now we're going to ride horses? In these mountains. In this snow. I've never even been on a horse in my life. Great! Just great!"

"What? What did you say?" asked John as he smiled over at Angelica.

"Huh? Oh, nothing. Nothing at all," responded Dex.

As they approached the corral, the two horses seemed to get extremely excited. They started running around, leaping in the air while kicking their back legs up so high that it looked as though they were trying to do some forward swiveling flip all the while making some strange snorting noise followed by a very intimidating loud whinny sounds. Their ears stood straight up, and the thick ungroomed hair on their backs seemed to come to life as it appeared bristly and untamed, resembling that of a wild animal. The three stood by the gate watching, not moving, not speaking, just watching as the two horses put on their display of enthusiasm.

"Well, what do you think?" asked an unsure John.

Without taking his eyes off the mighty horses, Dex replied in a shocked and hopeless tone, "I think you're crazy. You think I'm going to get on one of those things? No way."

"We have to get up there somehow," said John.

Dex turned away from the corral and looked up the steep mountain. He could easily see the mansion and how far it was. He leaned back against the fence and took a deep breath followed by a moment of silence and deep thought.

Then with a sudden sense of excitement, Dex lunged over at John, grabbing him in his arms, and said, "Hey, I got it. Let's walk up there!"

"What? You think we can make that walk?" replied John.

The two men turned away from the corral and took a long look at the steep terrain that led up to the mansion. They stood there wondering to themselves about the difficulty of making such a trip. It was either walk or try to ride the two overenthuaiastic horses, which neither man was too willing to try. When finally, John said, "I don't know. That's a long way up there. I don't know if we can make that walk."

As both men stood there contemplating over the trip, they heard a soft-spoken Angelica in the background talking in a whisper to the two horses. They turned to see Angelica stroking both horses on their foreheads and gently whispering to each. The horses appeared to be in some sort of calm-like state. Their eyes were glassy and rolled back. Their ears were flat as the horses went deeper into some relaxed state with each stroke of Angelica's hand.

"These animals don't even look like the same beasts from a minute ago. What did you do?" asked Dex.

"I just let them know that someone cares about them. That's all. They're fine now. You shouldn't have any problems getting these two to take you up to that mansion. Isn't that right?" she said to the horses as she continued to rub their foreheads.

"Wow. That's amazing," John said as he approached closer.

"They're not all that bad. Just a bit lonely out here is all. This one is named Herb," she said as she pointed to the one on her right. "And this one is named Rim Fire," she said as she looked to her left. "I told them to be gentle and take good care of both of you. They assured me that they would," she said as she smiled while continuing to stroke their foreheads.

"Say what?" replied Dex in amazement. "You mean, you can communicate with these animals?"

"Well, we're all God's creatures," she replied.

The two men looked at each other in disbelief, then slowly entered through the gate. The two horses gently followed John and Dex to the center of the corral. The horses stood quietly and patiently as the two men tried to figure out how to put on the saddles and bridles.

As the two mounted up on the horses, Dex asked Angelica, "Now what's the name of my horse again?"

"Rim Fire. His name is Rim Fire," she replied.

"Rim Fire. Oh, that's great! I'm sure he got that name for a reason," he said. "Hey, John, I have an idea. Why don't you ride Rim Fire, and I'll ride Herb?" asked Dex.

John smiled at Dex and said, "No, I think me and Herb have a connection already. I think he likes me. Look how gentle he seems. You'll be fine on that old worn-out Rim Fire," as he began to laugh.

"Yeah. Right!" said Dex.

Angelica said, "Remember, Dex, he's a lot older now," as she smiled. "You just need to hum to him now and then, especially when he starts getting excited. It calms him down."

Dex laughed and said, "Say what? Hum to him, like what? I don't know a lot of songs. Wasn't much of a music man." Dex started shaking his head as he began mumbling to himself. "Great. Just great. I can't believe I let you get me into these things."

"What was that? Did you say something?" asked John.

"No. No, I didn't say anything."

Angelica opened the gate and told the two men to be careful and do what they came here to do. "I'll be waiting," she said as the two men took off on horseback at a slow, steady, and uneventful pace.

"Hey, this isn't so bad. This is actually kind of fun," yelled John.

"Keep your voice down so you don't spook them," replied an uneasy Dex as he began to hum.

"Just let the horses show you the way. They know how to get up there," Angelica shouted as the two men waived back.

As the two men went on their way, you could hear Dex humming up a storm. He started off with a little AC/DC "Highway to Hell" but that didn't last very long. It seemed to excite old Rim Fire a bit. He quickly changed his tune and hummed a series of theme songs to TV shows he grew up watching, Like *Gilligan's Island* followed up by *The Brady Bunch*. Over and over, Dex hummed the theme songs, and it wasn't long before the two men reached the tree line and started their ascent up the mountain. Angelica stood near the corral and watched until they disappeared into the thick forest.

The two men didn't realize it at the time, but their adventure would now take them to an even more frightful series of events, events that would not only lead to answers about the case but events that would deeply affect both of their lives forever.

CHAPTER 22

The trail that led upward was dark and hard to see. The thick heavy limbs from the pine trees seemed to surround the men as they entered the forest. The mountain air was breezy, making the men nervous as the tree limbs that were draping over the trail seemed to come to life. The limbs swayed back and forth, sometimes violently as if they were trying to reach out to grab one of the men. Even though John and Dex were uneasy, the two horses acted as though they knew exactly where they were going and that nothing was out of the ordinary. John knew that with each gentle and careful step the two horses took on the snow-covered trail, they were getting closer and closer to the top.

As the two men went up the trail and got higher, they periodically took a look around to see the beauty of the valley. It was hard to realize how high and how quickly they had traveled. It was like looking down from the Empire State Building, only without a safety fence. Both men knew that one errant step or stumble from the horses while on the steep terrain could mean death by a horrible fall. So they didn't have much to say to one another as they journeyed up the trail. Instead, they kept to themselves, alone in their thoughts, but the view was breathtaking. All the while, Dex continued his humming as they rode.

It took the men about two nervous hours to reach the top. As the trail began to flatten out, the horses' heads suddenly came up. Their ears perked up sharply as if something had suddenly spooked them. They came to a dead stop, looking nervously around in all directions refusing to go any farther.

Dex leaned forward and quietly asked John, "What's going on?"

John, without looking back, whispered after a long pause, "I'm not sure. I think something scared them!"

"Shit. I hope there isn't a bear or something like that up there!" said Dex.

John leaned forward in his saddle so that he could take a look around a big tree limb that stretched out over the trail in front of him. There it was—the mansion. It was huge, like a giant standing there all alone and out of place in the wild and natural beauty of its surroundings. It was at least three stories tall, and it had a dark, eerie, abandoned look about it. The paint was peeling off in numerous places, revealing the grayish-brown wood underneath. To John, it was sad to see what was once a mighty, proud house standing tall in its surroundings, a house that would reflect a powerful man like Kenneth Daultry. But now, the house was a reflection of trouble. It was as though the mansion was absorbing the evil that was associated with Mr. Daultry.

Dex leaned forward and asked, "So what is it? What do you see?"

John turned slowly around to Dex and said, "This is it. Let's get off here. We can walk the rest of the way."

The two men tied the horses to some nearby trees, for they didn't seem too willing to go any further. It was as though the horses were trying to tell the two men that it wouldn't be safe to go on, but they had come this far, and they weren't going to turn around now.

As the two men walked up the remaining snow-covered slope in the trail, Dex began to see what John had seen, a towering, powerful-looking mansion in the middle of nowhere. It was surrounded by huge snow-filled evergreen trees with snowy drifts flanking the sides of the building. They approached slowly as they looked over every inch of the visible parts of the enormous structure. The breeze seemed to change into a steady wind that howled as it made its way through the trees and around the mansion. The wind began blowing the snow from off the ground and into the two men's faces.

With each step they took, they were getting closer and closer to the house, making the two men even more miserably cold. It wasn't a long walk from where the horses were tied up, but it seemed like it was an almost impossible task to get to the front door while fighting the unusual blizzardlike conditions. Dex began humming his theme songs again with every step.

John stopped, looked at Dex, and said, "Okay. You can stop the humming now. We're not on the horses."

Dex looked at John, shook his head, grinned, and said, "I know that. I-I just got used to humming I guess. It's no big deal. I can stop."

After the long journey from the bottom of the valley, the two men finally reached the front door. Neither have ever been so cold. Shivering and shaking, John reached his hand toward the doorbell. His hand was trembling with cold as he depressed the doorbell. They stood there waiting nervously, not saying much. They were just trying to get warm.

Suddenly, a loud out-of-place bang rang out that sent a nervous burst of energy through the two men. They quickly looked up to notice a shudder that had come loose in the heavy wind and was slapping violently against the building, almost as if the building itself had come to life and warned the two men to get away from this place while they still can. The shudder began to work its magic on Dex as he started pleading with John to leave and go back down to the resort. John just shook his head as he reached up for a second time to ring the bell.

Then before he could ring, the door jerked open. Standing in the doorway was a thin unhealthy-looking man with long gray hair that looked as though it hadn't been combed in a week. He moved slowly forward toward John and Dex. The shadows of the entry began to move across his face, giving him a mysterious, eerie look. Without saying a word, he moved even closer to the two men to get a better look. He squinted his eyes and frowned as he began looking the two men over. He then leaned forward and peeked out around the corner of the doorway as if he was nervous about something.

"I don't know you men," he said. "What are you doing out here? Are you two lost?"

"Well, I guess we are sort of," replied John.

"So you didn't answer my question. Why are you out here?"

"Uh, well, we were out here looking for the ski resort, and I guess we got turned around."

"Skiing, huh! Well, you're a little early. If it wasn't for this early blizzard, we wouldn't have any snow on the ground right now."

Quickly, John replied, "Yeah, I'm sure. You think we could come in and warm up? It's freezing out here."

"Well, I guess so. You guys better come in and get out of the weather. Come on in and get warmed up." John and Dex smiled and nodded as they began knocking the snow off their boots. "Come on. Hurry up and get in here so we can shut the door. This place gets cold, and it takes forever to get the chill out. Seems to always be cold in this place," he muttered.

He led the two men down a long dark corridor that led to a huge family room. The walls were filled with family portraits and trophies of the many animals that he had killed. A huge roaring welcoming fire seemed to provide an extra bit of warmth to the room, making Dex and John feel at ease.

"How about some coffee or hot tea?" Kenneth asked.

"Actually, coffee would be great," the two men replied.

"Okay, well have a seat by the fire, and I'll go make a pot."

Kenneth left the room, leaving John and Dex in the room alone. It gave them a chance to look around. They noticed that every light in the room was turned on. Flashlights and candles were scattered and sitting around everywhere. *That's strange,* thought John.

Dex said, "What is this guy afraid of—the dark?" in a soft tone.

John turned, looked at Dex, and said, "Yeah, I guess so."

After the two men warmed up, they began moving about the room, heading in different directions. At about the same time, they noticed one particular wall in the room. It didn't have the typical family portraits or trophy animals hanging on the walls at all. These pictures were different. The pictures were of Kenneth and his friends, happy and filled with life. Pictures of the many friends and expensive vacations that he had taken when he was younger. Pictures from his successful law practice and recognition awards that he had earned. The pictures told a story of a person who had a full life, nothing like the way he looked now. He seemed to be a broken-down paranoid man, alone and afraid.

As John scanned the many pictures on the wall, his attention was brought to one in particular, a picture that was off to the side, oddly out of place, and separated from the rest. It was a picture of Kenneth with five other people on a boat. It looked like it had been taken down at the resort below. It was a large boat with three couples, six friends standing arm and arm. All were having drinks and seemingly having a great time. In the background, you could see the resort: cabins, the lodge, the horse stables, and the horses. It was all laid out just as it appeared now. John looked in a little closer at the picture. His eyes focused on the boat, thinking to himself, *That looks exactly like the boat in my dream.* In the back of the boat was a brunette woman, the same woman from his dream that ended up in the water and was struck in the head with the oar.

Suddenly, Kenneth's voice rang out, "Hey, you guys want anything with your coffee—cream or sugar?"

"Black. Just black for me," replied John.

"Same for me," said Dex.

John whispered to Dex, "Hey, come here and look at this. That's the boat and that's the girl I saw in my dreams. He hit her in the head with an oar. He killed this girl and then left her down there in that lake somewhere."

Dex moved over to get a closer look. "You sure?" he asked.

"It's hard to recognize him, but this is Kenneth," he said as he pointed to the picture.

"No kidding. Man, has he changed. He doesn't look anything like he does now. Are you sure that is the girl?" asked Dex.

"Yes, I'm sure." John pointed to the two images in the picture and said, "That's Kenneth, and that's the girl who I saw in my dream. She was in the water, and he hit her over the head with the oar. I'm sure of it."

Suddenly, the doors from the kitchen flew open, and in walked Kenneth with a smile on his face, carrying a tray and three cups of coffee. As he entered the room, he looked up to find that John and Dex were looking at the picture. His smile quickly disappeared as he stopped.

"What are you guys doing?" he asked with a firm tone.

"Oh, we're just admiring all your pictures. You had quite an active life when you were younger," John said as Dex was nodding in agreement.

Kenneth stood there looking at the two men. He looked around the room somewhat nervously as if he were trying to figure out what to say, then he slowly made his way over to the coffee table.

He gently set the tray down, straightened back up, and said, "Yeah, I did back in those days. Tried to make the most out of my life, but those days are long gone. Now I just hang out up here. You see, I don't really like people very much anymore. Just can't trust anybody. Seems everybody is just out to GET YOU for one thing or another. No, I just keep to myself up here these days. Come and sit down and get your coffee."

John and Dex moved over to get their coffee as Kenneth moved to the fireplace to put more wood on the fire. Both men sat together on the couch as they watched Kenneth work on the fire. It was already blazing and very hot in the room, but Kenneth kept loading up the fire.

He turned and went over to his chair, saying, "I just can't get this place warm. It's always just so cold in this place. So tell me. How did you guys get up here, and where are you from?" he asked.

"We actually come from Boston. Just wanted to get out here and do some early skiing, but our car broke down on the way up here. So we walked to your house," replied John.

"Skiing. Well, you guys got lucky on that. We usually don't have this much snow for a couple of weeks yet. This is really a freak snowstorm," he said. "So what are your names?" he asked.

"I'm John, and this is Dex."

"Okay, John and Dex from Boston. Well, I'm Kenneth. Kenneth Daultry. So what do you guys do for a living? I'm a retired lawyer myself."

"Uh, marketing. I'm in marketing, and Dex here is in the research business," replied John.

"Research. That's a bit unusual. What kind of research do you do, Dex?"

Nervously, Dex said, "Marketing. Marketing research. I mean research marketing. We work together John and I. He's in marketing, and I research the market," as he laughed.

Kenneth sat back in his chair and crossed his arms. Looking suspicious, he asked, "So what is it that you research? I mean what sort of market would you be researching?"

John, realizing that Kenneth was beginning to get suspicious, quickly jumped in to rescue the conversation. "Starbucks! I identify promotional ideas for Starbucks based on Dex's expert research. I know you have heard of Starbucks. You know, the coffee business is very cutthroat these days and very competitive I might add," he said as both he and Dex nodded.

"I'm sure it is," replied Kenneth as he looked a bit curious.

With John's response, Kenneth leaned forward, nodded, and smiled, then took a sip of his coffee. John and Dex both seemed relieved that Kenneth seemed to believe their story.

The room grew increasingly uncomfortable and quiet as all three men just sat, sipping on their coffee. The occasional crack and pop from the fireplace was the only noise that broke the eerie silence.

John stood up and began moving around the room to break the tension while Kenneth sat back in his chair watching his every move.

"So you sure have a lot of pictures around here. Are you a professional photographer?" asked John.

"No. No, I've just always enjoyed taking a lot of pictures. A hobby I guess. It's amazing how many pictures a person can take through the years. Actually, I am a retired lawyer slash politician," he replied. "Each picture that you see is very special to me. Hard to believe so many years have passed. So many friends have come and gone. So many family members just gone. Sad. One day, you look around, and all you have left are these memories on a wall," he said.

In a way, John felt sorrow for Kenneth as he spoke about his friends and family that were no longer around, realizing that he, too, could relate to such loss while thinking about his own family. John, staring at the wall of pictures, fell into a deep trancelike state as he began remembering his last day that he spent with his son, throwing the football in his backyard before his last football game.

Suddenly, a loud pop from the fireplace seemed to snap John out of his trance. He noticed that the picture he was focused on was of Kenneth and his friends in a small boat. John moved up to the wall to get a closer look at the picture. It seemed familiar to him. It was a recognizable image that he had seen before. John, though feeling sorry for Kenneth, realized that their journey had led them to here and that Kenneth was a cold-blooded killer. He just has to get the evidence to put this guy away.

"So what's the story with this picture?" John asked as he pointed to the wall.

Kenneth stood up and moved closer to get a better look. He put on his glasses and leaned in, looking at the picture.

Kenneth, seemingly agitated, said, "Oh, that picture. Why would you ask about that picture?"

"No. No particular reason. You guys just seem to be having a great time. Was this picture taken down here at the resort? Who are these people? Let's see. Now that looks like you," John said as he pointed.

Kenneth became very irritated by John's questioning and responded hastily, "They're nobody special, just acquaintances. You know, people come and go around here all the time. Just some people I was showing a good time. I'm not even sure where any of these people are now. In fact, I thought I got rid of this picture a long time ago. You know, this is one of those pictures that I wished I had never taken," as he grinned. Without saying a word, Kenneth took the picture from the wall, crumpled it up into a small ball, and threw it in the fire. "There. All gone," he said as he wiped his hands across his chest.

John and Dex just watched as his domineer changed. They knew that they had touched a nerve by his strange behavior. Not wanting to raise any suspicions, the two men sat quietly while they watched Kenneth nervously move about the room. A sad and troubled look came over Kenneth's face as he seemed to be in heavy thought of a memory long gone.

"So you know it's cold out. This snowstorm is liable to dump a substantial amount of snow. It's going to be dark soon anyway, so you two might as well spend the night. I have plenty of room, but you guys will need to leave in the morning."

"Absolutely. Sure. First thing in the morning. That will be great," John replied.

With that said, the three men sat around for a while, having a general conversation and small talk over the next couple of hours. It was as if Kenneth just enjoyed having someone to share a conversation with. He prepared a food tray made up of expensive finger foods, dips, and various other things that weren't quite familiar with John and Dex. However, the two men were hungry, so they feasted on all the food anyway.

As the hours passed, Kenneth seemed to relax a bit and actually began feeling more comfortable with his newfound friends. John and Dex just let Kenneth talk as they sat and listened to his stories and adventures of years past. With each adventurous story, Kenneth's confidence grew, and his voice became stronger as he seemed to enjoy being the center of attention. John realized that this must be the true Kenneth as his powerful and controlling personality seemed almost threatening at times.

His tone began to rage as he started speaking of the many people that had crossed his path, almost as though he was bragging about how he got even with some of them and the terrible things he did to destroy some of their careers. Pointing at some of the pictures on the wall he said, "Friends. These are not my friends. They are just—"

Before he could finish, the clock struck midnight. The clock began to chime. Kenneth jumped back and turned around to look at the clock, just staring and listening. "Why, that clock hasn't chimed in years," he said with a stunned look. After the last chime sounded, a deafening quiet came over the room. Then suddenly, a door slammed from upstairs.

"Did you guys hear that?" asked Kenneth. The two men nodded.

"I thought you were alone in this house," John said.

Kenneth sat down in his chair and then leaned forward.

"Listen, I just want you both to know that there are things—unexplainable things—that have been happening in this house. It usually begins about this time of night."

Dex perked up and sat forward with a scared look on his face, saying, "Say what! Unexplained things! Like what kinda things?" He asked as he sat up and nervously looked around the room.

"Well, like the door slamming just now and all sort of things. Things out of place or things being moved without me moving it. It's been going on for a while, but it seems to be getting worse lately. I think this house has a ghost in it," replied Kenneth.

"What? Say what! Did you say a ghost? Oh, that's just great!" Dex said as he continued to look around the room.

Kenneth started to laugh and said, "Don't worry. You guys will be fine. Just stay in your rooms tonight, and nothing will happen to you. Besides, I think it's just after me." Kenneth smiled at the two men as he began moving closer to the fireplace. He looked down at the crackling fire in a gaze as he continued, "You see, the phone will ring sometimes at the oddest times late at night. You go to the phone and pick it up, and all you hear is this woman faintly crying. You ask who is it but just crying. I'll hang up, and a few moments later, the phone starts ringing again. It's the same thing for hours into the night. It just doesn't stop." Kenneth began to laugh, saying, "Hell, boys, I've even unplugged the phone. Guess what? It still rings!"

John and Dex took a big gulp of coffee as they turned to look at each other without saying anything. John then turned to Kenneth and asked, "So is the phone unplugged now?"

"Go ahead and check," he replied.

John walked over to the phone and picked up the receiver—no dial tone.

"Yup, it's unplugged all right," he said as he put the phone down.

"I keep it unplugged all the time now unless I need to call out, but it really doesn't matter. She'll call when she wants."

Suddenly, a loud banging started coming from outside that startled John and Dex to the point they almost spilled their coffee.

"What the heck is that?" asked Dex.

"Shutters. I have a few loose wooden shutters outside. When the wind picks up, they really get after it out there, man," Kenneth said as he smiled. "I've always meant to get those things fixed but just haven't gotten around to it."

Dex took a deep breath and looked around the room as he said, "Well, I would be getting those things fixed first thing in the morning if I were you."

Kenneth chuckled, knowing the two men were scared and then he continued, "You know, I probably shouldn't be telling you all this stuff, but I just don't get many visitors up here. Ah, what the heck? I'll tell you anyway."

John and Dex sat down as they both had a tight hold on their coffee cup.

Kenneth continued, "So I came down to the kitchen one morning about a week ago I suppose. Well, when I opened the door, I noticed this grungy woman dripping with water. She was just sitting there at the table. She looked sort of familiar I guess, but it was hard to tell. The lights were not on, and she was just sitting there, not saying a word by a flickering candle. It was like she was just waiting for something. I guess she was waiting for me now that I think back. I flipped on the light, and this thing stood up and looked over at me. It was grotesque. She had black hair with what looked like green vines tangled throughout her hair. Her skin and face were unreal and distorted to the point she was difficult to look at.

"That's when she came right up to me. Well, I was frozen with fear and couldn't move. She got right up to my face and opened her mouth. It was a disgustingly foul odor. Then she said to me, 'I'll be waiting for you.'

"After that, she turned away and left the kitchen through a back set of stairs that leads upstairs. I finally got my senses back and went up the stairs after her, but she was nowhere to be found. I looked all over this house, never did find her, and I hope I don't ever see her again."

John and Dex sat there looking at Kenneth. He wasn't smiling anymore but rather had a serious look on his face. "So you see what I've been dealing with around here." Kenneth moved over to the staircase leading upstairs. Just before he headed up the stairs, though, he stopped and looked back at the two men who were in disbelief and were quietly just sitting there, watching Kenneth. Kenneth said to the two, "Well, guys, I'm going to bed. Find a room upstairs. There's plenty, but whatever you do, just stay there. Don't come out no matter what you hear in this house. Just stay in your rooms."

CHAPTER 23

As Kenneth went upstairs, John and Dex stood up and moved over to the bottom of the stairs, looking up. A strange and uncomfortable feeling came over both of them. It was like a cold blast of air that instantly moved through them, giving them a deep chill that shook their core.

Suddenly, the lights in the room all went out. The only light came from the flickering soft lights of the candles that had been sat out around the room. They began noticing shadows on the walls all around the room, moving about with the flickering lights from the candles. The shadows on the walls seemed to come to life, working together as they began creating strange, distorted, and eerie images. The two men stood in silence and uneasiness as they watched the shadow images come together, creating more deliberate and recognizable shapes. It was as if the shadows were coming together creating a storyboard on the walls for the two men to watch, much like a black-and-white film.

They could clearly see a boat in the water and what looked like a man and a woman having an argument of some kind on the deck of the boat. The man began hitting the woman several times and then pushed her overboard. The woman reached for the boat and tried to get back on board several times, but the man kept blocking her and pushing her back down in the water. Finally, he reached for an oar and hit her over the head as she tried one last time to get back on the boat. Her body went still as she slipped down into the darkness of the water. Then suddenly and slowly, the shadows on the walls began to move and break apart, leaving the normal flickering of the candlelight on the walls.

John looked over at Dex. "Wow. That was brutal," he said with a soft tone.

"But that's it. That's what I saw in my dream."

"I think this happened down here at the resort," he said.

As the two stared at the wall thinking about what they just saw, a new set of images began to emerge from the shadows. *Now what?* they thought. As the new images came together, they could recognize the resort below. The layout was the same: the lodge, the cabins, horse barn, and stables. They were all there. Then the shadows began to show a car driving up and stopping at the well, which was located in the center of the resort. The shadows showed a man getting out of the car and moving to the trunk of the car. He popped the trunk, reached in, and pulled out the lifeless body of a young woman.

"I think that's her," John said quietly.

"That's who?" asked Dex.

"I think that may be our missing art student, the whole reason we are here," he said.

The two men sat quietly and watched as the scene continued to play out. The man from the car carried the girl over to the well, laid her on the wall of the well, and pushed her in. With that, the shadows on the wall faded, and the images were gone like before.

John, with excitement, slapped Dex on the arm and said, "That's it. She's in the well. He bought this place after disposing of her body and shut it down so nobody would discover her body."

"But what about the girl on the boat. Who's that?" asked Dex.

"She must have found out about our art student. That's the only thing that makes sense. She probably confronted Kenneth about it and told him she was going to the authorities, but Kenneth didn't want any part of that. So he took her out on that boat late one night and killed her too. Her body has to be out there on the bottom of that lake somewhere. Neither one of these girls have ever been found. I'm not sure who this other girl is, but we need to find out and get her back to her family. This guy Kenneth is a bad dude. He killed these two girls, closed this place down, and has been living up here in isolation all these years. We need to be careful tonight in case he decides to come after us. We should take turns sleeping just in case."

"I agree and don't forget about the pissed-off ghost. I think it's the girl from the boat," said Dex.

"Yeah, well, you may be right, but I don't think she's pissed at us. Now Kenneth, on the other hand, she's pissed at him for sure. I think she's been haunting him for years. He looks like he's been tormented by her. He looks a lot older than he really is," replied John.

With that, the two men moved upstairs and soon found themselves in a dark hallway. They slowly moved down the hall checking the rooms. They wanted to find a room large enough that had two beds so they could stay together. Dex looked down the hall and noticed an image of someone standing there in the dark at the far end of the hallway.

"Hey, you see that?" he said as he nudged John on the shoulder.

John focused down the hall and said, "Yes, I do."

The two men moved closer to the image. It was Kenneth, just standing in a dark corner of the hall. He seemed to be watching their every move.

"Hey, guys, did you find a room?" he asked.

"No, not yet," replied John.

"Oh, okay, well, let me help. Try this one here," he said as he pointed to a door down the hall.

The room was a large one, just what they were looking for. In no way were they going to separate for the night. There were two beds, and they both sat down at about the same time. They looked at each other and took a deep breath as they tried to make sense of what had been happening.

Both John and Dex had been doing police work for years. So they knew that they couldn't just go to the authorities with their stories of dreams, ghosts, and shadow images on the walls. No, they would be laughed out of the police station, especially knowing that they were accusing some high-powered attorney like Kenneth with his local family influence. John looked over at Dex. He could tell he was exhausted.

"You know, Dex, we are on our own with this thing. The authorities aren't going to take any of this seriously. No, we are going to have to solve this on our own. We've got to get some evidence, hard physical evidence."

"Yes, I was afraid you were going to say that, but you're right," Dex replied.

"So what are you thinking?" asked Dex.

"I'm thinking we get a little bit of rest. I'll stay up and keep watch. You get some sleep for about an hour, then we will switch. We both need some rest. It was just a little strange, Kenneth standing in the hall like that. I don't trust that he believes who we are. I think he is still trying to figure us out. Once we know he's asleep, we can look around. He may have a journal, a diary, pictures, or anything that can identify these two women and who they were."

"Okay, sounds good," said Dex as he got up from the bed and headed toward the bathroom. "Hey, I think I may take a quick hot shower."

John lay back in the bed and relaxed as Dex took his shower. The shower was huge. It was a steam/shower spa of some sort, large enough for three or four people. He had never been in a shower this big. "Man, you have to see this shower," shouted Dex.

As the hot water hit the cold air, thick steam and fog began to fill the bathroom, making it hard for Dex to see anything around him. The steam and fog were thick, and it wasn't long before the walls began to disappear from his vision. "Wow, this is great. You're going to love this," he shouted again.

Dex began lathering up with soap and relaxing as the hot water poured over his body. *Man, this is just great,* he thought to himself. Suddenly, he noticed an unfamiliar odor, a foul, pungent smell that filled the shower. *What the heck?* he thought. *What is with this water?* Dex cupped his hands to catch some of the water from the shower and took a deep smell. "Hmm, that seems okay, not really smelling anything in the water. It must be the drain pipes I guess. He really needs to get these things cleaned out," he said to himself. As Dex continued with his shower, the pungent odor only got worse.

"Hey, John, did you come in here and take a dump while I was showering? Man, you got to warn somebody when you do that. Wow! You know, you need to add some fiber to your diet. Try some Metamucil every once in a while. That helps me," Dex said as he laughed, but he heard no reply from John.

The bad smell began to worsen until he decided to turn off the water. *Man, I just can't take it anymore,* he thought to himself. With the water turned off, the steam began to lower, but the strong odor only got worse and more intense. *Wow, this is horrible,* he thought. *I got to get out of here.* Dex began to cough

226

as his throat began to close up, making it hard to get any air.

As the steamy air began to thin, he noticed the image of someone behind him on the far wall of the shower. He rubbed his eyes as if he were clearing his vision to get a better look. The strong odor only got worse, now smelling like rotten and decaying flesh. The image then moved rapidly and lunging toward Dex from the back wall. Dex jumped back and said, "What the hell?"

He quickly jumped out of the shower, grabbed his clothes, and ran out into the room where John was lying in bed. John jumped up as Dex started backing up out of the bathroom while holding his clothes against his naked body and pointing toward the bathroom door. John looked over at the door as Dex was standing there, panting and trying to catch his breath.

"What's going on?" asked John.

"Sh-Sh-Sh-Shit!" Dex responded as he was pointing toward the bathroom.

The steam from the shower began to spill out into the room as the two stood there, watching the bathroom door. Slowly, the silhouette of a woman began to emerge in the doorway. As she moved forward, the two men were frozen in fear. She had long dark hair on one side of her head, but on the other side, her head looked as though it were caved or bashed in. Her hair on that side was folded down around the side of her face, revealing her skinless bashed-in skull and protruding eye. Her skin was rotten with yellow, black, and green blotches all over her body and reeking like dead and decaying flesh. As the woman moved closer, they realized it was the girl from the boat. She didn't seem to acknowledge either of them as she floated across the room and passed through the closed door and into the hallway. The two men looked at each other and then ran over to the door.

John grabbed the door handle as Dex said, "Wait a minute. Kenneth said to stay in our rooms and not to come out no matter what we see or hear."

"It's too late for that. She came to us," he replied.

John pulled open the door as the two men followed her out into the hallway. They watched as she slowly glided down the hall toward Kenneth's room and then she was gone. The two men stood next to each other, looking down the hall to see if she would reappear.

"Where did she go?" asked Dex in a very soft tone.

"I don't know. She just disappeared," he replied.

"Geez, have you ever seen anything like that before?" Dex asked.

"No, but I've seen a lot of things lately that I can't explain."

Suddenly, the two men heard a high-pitched scream coming from Kenneth's room at the end of the hallway. It wasn't a woman screaming but sounded like a very frightened Kenneth. Then the sound of two shots being fired followed by another set of screams from Kenneth.

John turned to Dex and said, "Go get our guns now." Dex turned to get their guns from their rooms while John stayed in the hallway watching Kenneth's door to his room. Then the door flew open as Kenneth came backing out of his room and into the hallway. He fired two more shots aimlessly into his room as he kept backing up, then again with another shot.

The woman appeared and came out into the hallway from Kenneth's room. Kenneth turned and took off, running down the hall toward John. Kenneth ran up to John and stopped. He was panting heavily while trying to catch his breath.

"Can you see her?" he asked John.

"Yeah," replied John as he shook his head.

Kenneth began reloading his gun as the woman stood at the other end of the hallway, not saying anything but just staring at Kenneth. Then she pointed at the two men as she began slowly gliding toward them. Kenneth aimed his gun and fired again, but it didn't seem to slow her down. She just kept coming. By now, Dex had returned to the hallway and handed John his gun.

Kenneth looked at Dex as he handed John his gun and said, "Guns. You guys have guns? Well, good then. Let's all unload on her. Maybe that will make her go away."

John looked over at Kenneth and with a smile on his face, said, "I don't think so. This is your problem, not ours."

The woman seemed to start moving faster toward the men with her focus on Kenneth. As the girl got closer, Kenneth started backing up down the hallway while John and Dex stood still at the door to their room, not moving as they watched her pursue Kenneth. As the girl passed by John and Dex, Kenneth kept backing up as he began to panic. He started firing his gun in a futile effort to stop her, but she seemed to be relentless in her pursuit. As Kenneth backed up, he found himself at the edge of the steep stairs that led down to the lower part of the house. In a split second, she moved instantly to Kenneth's face. She said in an evil tone to Kenneth, "I've been waiting!"

With his back to the stairs, Kenneth jumped back with fright, lost his footing, and fell hard down the stairs tumbling end over end until he reached the bottom. John and Dex raced over to the rail and looked down to find Kenneth lying at the bottom of the stairs. The lights from the candles in the lower room showed Kenneth's broken and motionless body.

"I think he's dead," said Dex.

"Yeah, I would say so," John replied.

John and Dex looked over at the woman who was still standing at the top of the stairs. Her attention left Kenneth whose broken body was lying at the bottom of the stairs. She slowly turned her head and looked over at the two men. Then she turned and began moving slowly toward the two men. Dex cocked his gun and started to raise it up to aim, but John grabbed his arm and pushed it back down. "It won't do any good. Just stand strong and don't back up," John said.

The two men stood firm as the woman moved closer. Her appearance began to change, and the foul odor that came with her seemed to subside. As she got closer, she evolved into this beautiful woman with long flowing brunette hair and penetrating sparkling, crystal-blue eyes. John and Dex's fear was eased as they realized she was the woman from the boat that Kenneth bashed with the oar.

She slowly moved up to the two men, smiled, and leaned forward to say in a soft whisper, "Check his desk. You'll find the answers you've been looking for in his desk." She stepped back away from the two men, smiled, and slowly faded away.

CHAPTER 24

The two men had a huge sense of relief and felt like the worst was over. They hurried down the stairs to check on Kenneth. He hadn't moved or made any noise since he had fallen down the stairs. John kneeled down over him and checked for a pulse or any signs of a breath. There was none. They knew that Kenneth had met his frightful demise, and it upset John to think that he would never be brought to justice, though he would face justice of another kind where he was heading. Knowing that his final judgment was now ahead of him gave John some sense of satisfaction. He slowly rose up over Kenneth and looked at Dex.

"Now let's go find that desk of his!" he said.

"Yup, let's do it," replied Dex.

John said, "She said to check his desk that the answers we seek were in his desk."

The two men went from room to room in the big house, searching every desk that they came across but couldn't find any information to help their case against Kenneth. The remainder of the evening flew by as the two men searched the house, and soon, the sun would be coming up.

Exhausted and frustrated, John yelled out to Dex, "Hey, have you found anything?"

"No. No, but I'm not exactly sure what I'm looking for," responded Dex.

"There's got to be something. Either we missed it or we just haven't found the right desk yet," said John.

Dex walked up to John about then and told him that he was exhausted. John agreed, and both men decided to take a break. They went to the kitchen, made some coffee, and sat down. Neither had much to say to one another. Both were just extremely tired and just sat and drank their coffee.

About fifteen minutes passed before Dex started talking, "So you know that if we don't find anything to support what happened here, the authorities are going to think we killed this guy. Shit! That would just top off this whole thing."

John started laughing. "Yeah, you are probably right about that. That would make the whole trip. That would just be a heck of a thing."

With that, John took a long pause as if he just thought of something. Dex had seen that look on John's face before. Usually, it was when he asked Dex to do something that he knew Dex really didn't want to do or he thought of something that might help their case.

John looked over at Dex with a twinkle in his eye, saying, "Didn't Kenneth tell us about a set of stairs that led out of the kitchen, a set of stairs that led to the upper part of the house?"

"Yeah, he sure did. He told us about them when he was telling us about the girl in the kitchen," replied Dex.

"So where are the stairs?" asked John.

Both men stood up from the table and looked around the kitchen. There were no stairs to be seen. The only way into the kitchen was through the doors they came in from.

"Well, that's weird," Dex said as he scratched his head.

"Just look around the walls. I'm saying there's a hidden doorway in here somewhere. There's got to be."

The two men began pushing on the walls and moving anything that they could, trying to find the stairway. They started on opposite sides of the kitchen and worked their way around the room until they meet up at an old potbelly stove. John looked down and saw a large handle on the corner of the stove. He reached down, grabbed the handle, and pulled. The stove began to move, swinging freely and easily, revealing a hidden stairway. John looked over at Dex and then the two men quickly made their way up the stairs. Three flights of stairs they went up, all the way to the third level of the house. At the top was a huge hidden office.

As they walked through the doorway, they noticed all kinds of award and recognition plaques that he had earned from his high school swim team, community recognition, and involvement awards to cases that he had won over the years. The room was also filled with family photos and pictures from their law firm along with vacations with friends that he had taken over the years. Yes, Kenneth had a full life, and it was sad to realize that he had thrown all that away, knowing what he had become. The two men gathered themselves after taking a few moments to see the awe of the room.

In the center of the room was a huge but beautiful mahogany desk. John moved to behind the desk and sat down in Kenneth's soft, plush leather chair. In front of him was a small, thin drawer located at the top center of the desk. He slowly pulled out the drawer and laid it on top of the desk. John began pulling out items as they both looked at each item, knowing this was Kenneth's private and personal life. They carefully went through every drawer in the desk but found nothing that would incriminate Kenneth for these murders.

"It's got to be here. Somehow we've missed it or just not seeing it," said a frustrated John.

"Maybe there's another desk somewhere," replied Dex.

"No, I don't think so. It's got to be here. We are just not seeing it."

John then picked up the small drawer that they searched first, held it up, and quickly banged himself in the forehead with frustration.

Dex was shocked but then became very excited as he said, "Hey, do that again!"

"Say what?" replied John.

"Do that again. No, not the headbutt thing. Just flip over the drawer."

John turned over the drawer and laid it on the desk. Taped underneath the drawer was an envelope. On it read, "Property of Kenneth Daultry. If anything happened to me, please read upon my death."

John pulled off the envelope and opened it. In it were four handwritten pages. He began reading the documents out loud to Dex. It described his torment, his feelings of guilt, and how he had hidden the truth of what he had done from his family, his friends, and the authorities for all these years.

The letters described the death of two women and how he accidentally killed his true love when he was in college, a young college student named Susan Ashworth. She was a young talented art student in Boston with a promising career, but one night in a heated argument, she fell on a sculpturing tool while trying to get away from him. The letter said how she died as he held her in his arms. He then panicked and didn't know what to do. So he wrapped her body up in a blanket and drove her to Denver in his car, bringing her out here to the resort where his family always vacationed. Not knowing what to do with her, he ended up dumping her body in the well, hoping that she would never be found, and he would never be found responsible for her death. He just walked away from the whole thing as if she never existed.

The second woman was a friend that liked to come along with his group of friends. Her name was Brittani Stephans. She liked to party, but she was a bit wild. No one else from his group of friends gave her much attention because of her wild side, but she was a lot of fun to be around.

The incident that Kenneth described was that one night after partying on the boat, the two were alone. She started telling Kenneth about all her troubles in her life, and sometimes she just felt all alone. She just didn't seem to have family support, and no one seemed to care about her.

Kenneth, being somewhat drunk, began to open up to Brittani and let his guard down. Since she was telling him of her hardships, he thought he could tell her of his. He told her about Susan, his old love from college and that she had accidentally died in his arms after they had an argument. He went on and told her where he had put her—in the well. He didn't anticipate Britani's reaction and that was when things went terribly wrong.

She started telling him that they needed to contact the police and get her home with her family. Kenneth knew then he had made a mistake in telling her. Their relationship was never the same after that. He said that she didn't look at him with the same interest as she had before.

As their relationship continued to get worse, he knew that it was a matter of time before she went to the police. So he invited her out to the resort alone. They got in the boat and went out to the far end of the lake. There, they got into a heated argument where she said she would be going to the police. So he pushed her overboard and hit her in the head with an oar until she was dead. He tied her up, attached a boat anchor with a rope to her legs, and then watched her sink into the darkness of the lake. He told his friends that she wouldn't be coming around anymore and that she had moved away so they wouldn't be asking about her.

After that, he bought the resort and closed it down. The letter closed with an apology to the girls and their families, saying that he was terribly sorry but never asked for forgiveness. He finished by saying that he is leaving the entire resort and his house to Charles, the old caretaker at the resort.

After reading the letter, John leaned back in the chair and laid the letter down on the desk. A smile slowly came over his face as he looked up at Dex and then it quickly went away when he realized the tragedy of these events.

"Well, this is it. This is all we need. We can contact the authorities, find these two girls, and get them back to their families," said John.

John leaned forward in the chair and reached for the phone, hoping there was a dial tone. Remarkably, there was, so he dialed 911. It wasn't long before the authorities arrived. They read Kenneth's letter and listened to John and Dex's story of the events from the past several days. John told them everything that he knew the police would understand, everything that was believable. So he left out the parts about the ghosts.

After they secured Kenneth's body, the team of police officers, John, and Dex, made their way down to the resort. John and Dex looked around for Angelica, but she was nowhere to be found. She was just gone. The old Indian Charles came out of the barn with the two horses.

Charles said, "Good to see you guys made it back okay. What did you do to bring the whole police force with you?"

"Yeah, pretty much. Charles, you wouldn't believe what we've been through," replied John. "Oh, by the way, Mr. Daultry is dead."

"What did you guys do—go up and kill my boss? Well, there goes my paycheck," he said.

John said, "No. No, we didn't kill the guy. But guess what? You now own this place. You are your own boss, and you can reopen and rebuild this place the way it was before."

"Get out of town!" said Charles. "My own boss. Wow. My own boss," he kept saying to himself as he walked away, leading the horses to the barn.

John and Dex remained in Colorado for several more days while helping the authorities find the girls' bodies and close down the case. Angelica never did come back to the resort, and John worried about her. He wondered what happened to her and why she wasn't waiting for them like she said she would. However, it was a good feeling that the two men had when they realized that the families of these two girls could now be at peace and find closure for their missing loved ones who were now going to be returned to their homes thanks to John and Dex.

Susan Ashworth's body was found in the well, just like Ken had stated in his note. However, it took a little longer to find the remains of Brittani who was found in the deep end of the lake. Her skeletal remains had a rope tied to her legs and boat anchor that was attached to the other end. For John and Dex, they could now finally start to relax, knowing that this case had been solved and knowing they could finally return home to Boston.

CHAPTER 25

The two men grabbed a flight home from Denver back to Boston. For John, the flight was relatively uneventful, but for Dex, however, the flight home may have turned out to be everything he dreamed of. Almost immediately when they boarded the flight, a young red-haired, green-eyed stewardess took notice to Dex. As Dex walked past her, she winked at him, gave him a big welcoming hug, and then showed him to his seat. Dex wasn't sure what to make of the situation, but when she showed him her big inviting smile, he definitely took notice.

John sat down in his seat, sat back, and watched with amusement while Dex started nervously fumbling around in response to her flirtatious behavior. She seemed to be giving Dex the gold-star treatment with an excessive amount of attention followed by what one would consider I-want-you-bad amount of pampering. She had purposely left the seat open next to Dex who was sitting by the window and, on several occasions throughout the flight, would come and sit next to Dex, giving him a sampling of things to come. After each somewhat-ravaging event, Dex would glance over at John with a smile on his face as if he was looking for John's approval.

Dex had never truly had a real relationship with a woman. Being plagued with a stuttering problem his entire life, he was never looked at as the strong, confident type. Most of the women that Dex showed an interest in simply walk away from him once he started talking. However, this was different, Dex was no longer stuttering, and she wasn't walking away.

It made John feel like a proud father of sorts as if he were watching his son showing interest in girls for the first time. John couldn't help feeling happy for his friend, but at the same time, he started thinking about his own family. He lay his head back on the headrest, closed his eyes, and tried to vision his family in his mind. It was sad for him to realize that he would never get to share this sort of experience with his own son. Sadly, as time went by, it seemed to be getting more and more difficult for him to picture his family in his mind. The loss of those visions in his mind of his family only deepened his sadness.

As the plane landed, John quickly got up out of his seat, leaving Dex and his newfound girlfriend who were showing no signs of cooling off and exited the plane. John headed down to the baggage-claim area, picked up his luggage, and waited for his friend.

After about fifteen minutes, Dex came walking up. His hair was a mess and all out of place. His lips were swollen, which gave off a fiery-red glow. It looked as though he had scratches on the side of his face and back of his neck. His shirt was half untucked and missing two top buttons.

"Wow, man, what happened to you? Did that little stewardess do all this to you? You look like you've really been roughed up," John asked as he began to laugh.

"Oh yeah, man! And it was great. I've never experienced anything like that," he replied.

"Well, from what I saw, I don't know many people that have experienced anything like that. So did you get her name?" he asked.

"Ashley. Her name is Ashley. Look, she gave me her number, and she wants to get together and go out tonight," he said as he showed John her number. "She lives here in Boston."

John glanced at the number and said, "Well, be careful. Don't let her hurt you. She seems like a rough little player."

Dex responded, saying, "Oh no. No, she just has a lot of passion. No, we are just going to take it slow for now. You know, get to know each other a little better."

"Slow. Yeah, right," John replied with laughter.

The two men grabbed their luggage and headed outside. It wasn't long before a taxi pulled up. Dex told John to go ahead and take this one and he would take the next one since they were heading in two different directions.

They shook hands as John asked, "Well, I guess this is it. So what are you planning on doing next?"

"Oh, hadn't thought about it. I guess I might just go back to selling cars. How about you?"

John looked out across the area in front of him and said, "Not sure either. Guess I'll just take it easy for a while and see what comes my way."

With that, John loaded his bags in the taxi, got in, closed the door, and rolled down the window as the taxi began to drive off. John stuck out his hand and gave Dex a thumbs-up. He said as he was driving off, "What an adventure we had. Now go get that girl."

Dex's eyes began to water as he yelled back, "Hey, if you ever need me for anything, if you ever need my help with another case, just give me a call. I'll be there."

About six months had passed since he left Dex at the airport. There had been nothing new or anything of interest for John to keep his thoughts from his family. He kept wondering about Angelica, where she went, and what happened to her, hoping that he might run across her or hear from her, but he never did. Getting bored, he opened his windows no matter how cold it may be outside in the hopes that maybe those strange birds would come back, but they never did either.

John began walking around the neighborhood simply to get out of his apartment. He had no friends, no one to talk to. It was as if he was a stranger in his own town, no one to help occupy his time. He was simply alone.

One day, John decided to open up his box of family photos. He pulled them out and separated them by laying them out on the coffee table. He sat there and gazed over his keepsakes: pictures, birthday cards, and personal notes from his family. The memories came flooding back as he began to weep. John was becoming more and more depressed with each passing day as this became his daily routine.

Late one afternoon while John was on a walk through the neighborhood, he realized that he was only a few blocks away from the old bar that he used to go to. It was where he hung out before meeting Angelica. He thought to himself, *I should just go in there and have a drink. It's been a long time, and I haven't had a drink in a while. One drink won't hurt anything.*

He stopped, looked around as if he was worried that someone might be watching him, and then he began heading toward the bar. As he walked closer, he could see the sign hanging just over the edge of the street. "Omally's Bar," it said with its fluorescent blinking sign that acted like a beacon and welcomed all hardy Bostonian bar-goers. Tall buildings towered over both sides of the street that he really hadn't noticed before, and as the sun began going down, darkness quickly filled the street.

One by one, the streetlights began to flicker and turn on for the night. Up ahead, one in particular that stood on a street corner began to turn on. As the light grew brighter, the silhouette of a woman standing underneath the streetlamp began to emerge. John stopped, squinted his eyes, and took a harder look. "Angelica," he said to himself. His heart started pounding and his excitement grew as he thought that this could be her.

He quickly moved up to her. And yes, it was her. She looked at John and smiled as he came closer. The light from the streetlamp that fell around her made her look more beautiful and more majestic than ever. They gave each other a tight embrace as John told her that he was so happy to see that she was okay and that he has been worried about her.

He stepped back away from her after their embrace and asked, "So where have you been? We came back down from Kenneth's place. You said you would be waiting for us, but you were gone. Do you have any idea how worried I've been? No note, no nothing. You just left."

She said, "I know. I'm sorry, but I had to leave. I had faith that you and Dex would be okay and find the truth about the missing girls." Angelica reached over, touched John on the arm, and said, "You know, you and Dex make a great team. You two did a wonderful job finding those two girls and returning them to their families. They are now at peace. They wanted me to let you know how much they appreciate what you did and to say thank you."

John looked a little puzzled and confused at what she just said. "Say what? They wanted you to tell me thank-you?" he asked.

She touched him again on the arm as she looked deep into his eyes. A calmness began to surge over him as she started to speak, "So let me explain. I'm not who or what you think I am. I'm what you call a spiritual muse. I'm here to help people like you, people that have lost their way, people that feel like their purpose in life has left them and those that have lost their faith. You see, John, you helped those two girls and their families to find closure. Because of you, those two girls are where they are supposed to be, in a better place. By you helping them, you also helped yourself, both you and Dex. You see, John, there is a better place, a great place, a wonderful place, a place full of passion and forgiveness. It's a place where people in spirit form go once you pass beyond this world. It's a place where loved ones are waiting for us all. Your family is there, waiting for you now, and someday, you will all be together again."

"But I want to be with my family now. I miss them so much. I just don't know what to do. I just don't know if I can go on. What am I going to do?" he asked.

Angelica took his hand and continued, "I know it's hard to believe, but things happen for a reason. You have a purpose in life. Your time in this world is not complete yet, and you, like me, are here to help others. So you must go on. You still have too much to do in this world. You won't know when, where, or how. It will just happen, but you will know when it's time to help. I know it's hard losing loved ones, but one day, you'll all be together again."

With those final words, Angelica smiled at John and stepped back under the streetlamp as her image began to fade. John could only watch until she completely disappeared. John stood there in disbelief as she faded away, but at the same time, he felt the heaviness of his depression begin to lift. *Did she really just disappear in front of my eyes?* he thought to himself. *If she can do that, then it must be real. There must really be a place that we go after we are done with this life.* Tears began to fall down his face as he turned away from the bar.

Overcome with emotion, his depression was gone and replaced with a new sense of peace and hope. He wiped away his tears and decided to go home. He felt like he had things he had to do and wanted to get a good night's rest.

The next morning, John woke to the sounds of bird wings fluttering nearby. He sat up to see his old friend—that strange little bird that kept him company after his family was murdered. "Well, hello there, little guy. Where have you been?" he asked.

The bird let out a couple of squawks and began fluttering up and down to John's delight. John gave him a few pieces of torn bread as he sat back and watched his little friend. The morning sunlight came beaming through his window that seemed to not only wake up his apartment but gave John a new vigor for life. He sat back and thought, *What do I need to do today? Coffee. I definitely need to start the day with coffee.* John shaved, got dressed, and headed for his favorite coffee shop.

In some way, the people he saw along the way seemed friendlier and much happier. Even the people at the coffee shop seemed much more talkative. He sat at the restaurant wondering to himself what to do next. Then suddenly, he thought, *The priest. I need to go see the priest. Last time I was there, I didn't leave on good terms.*

John left the coffee shop and headed toward the church where he had had the confrontation with the priest. It was one of the oldest churches in the area with a magnificent towering cathedral that overlooked the street below. He walked up the stairs leading to the entrance door and pushed open the massive doors. He slowly walked into the main room, and it wasn't hard to see the priest standing in front of the altar. It was as if he was waiting for someone to arrive.

John quietly approached the priest. He seemed to remember John as he smiled and then opened his arms, inviting him to come forward. "How can I help you son?" he asked.

The two sat down in front of the altar as John told the priest his story. The priest listened intently as he described the way he had lost his family and himself from beginning to end. He told him about Angelica and the incredible events associated with her and what she had told him. Then John apologized for what he had said to him earlier.

"It's not true—what I said a while back. I know now that there is something out there, somewhere we go after this world. I know that now," John said.

The priest stood up and told John that he forgave him, then he blessed him and said, "Son, there are many things that happen that don't make sense when they happen, but there is a reason. We can't always understand it at first, but there is a plan. It sounds to me that you have been chosen. For what? Only you will know when it's time."

John left the priest feeling like a heaviness had been lifted off his shoulders. As he left, he just started walking away from the church with no real direction in mind. It wasn't long before he found himself back at the park from a few months ago. He looked around and found a familiar face. It was the young boy he had played catch with in the park before.

"Hey. Hey, kid. You remember me?" shouted John.

"Sure," replied the boy as he motioned for John to come over.

The boy had a big smile on his face as the two began to throw a football back and forth. It was a great sunny day. John began noticing the sounds around him, like birds chirping and children laughing all about, sounds that he hadn't noticed in a while.

"So, kid, what's your name?" asked John.

"Timmy. My name is Timmy," he replied.

"Oh, okay. That's a cool name."

"What is your name?" asked the boy.

"It's John. My name is John O'Roark."

"Okay, cool," said the boy.

"So are you out here by yourself?" asked John.

"No. My mom and sister are over by the swings," he responded.

The two kept throwing the ball back and forth for a while longer.

"I really appreciate you throwing the ball with me, John. I used to do this with my dad all the time.

We would come to the park and do exactly what we are doing right now."

"Is that right? I used to do the same with my son in our backyard," John replied. "So where is your dad at? Is he at work or something?" asked John.

"No, not really sure. He's been gone for a while. Hey, you want to come over and meet my mom?" he asked.

"Sure, kid, I'll meet your mom," replied John.

The young boy came over, grabbed John by the hand, and led him over to the swing sets. His mom was sitting there as she watched her daughter on the swings. John began to see what looked like his little bird friends from his apartment. They were on top of the swing set just watching.

As John got closer, the two birds let out a squawk and flew off into the trees. *That's weird*, he thought. They walked up to his mom who was sitting on the park bench while watching her daughter.

Timmy said, "Hey, Mom, there is someone I want you to meet. We've been playing catch."

"Hello, I'm Jennifer," she said as she held out her hand. "And who are you?" she asked.

"John. John O'Roark," he replied.

Jennifer's eyes grew wide and then began to water upon hearing John's name.

"John," she said. "I believe I've been waiting for you!"

The End

ABOUT THE AUTHOR

William L. Harben is the author of *I've Been Waiting* and is a graduate of Texas Tech University. He is a longtime teacher and coach who has always had a knack for telling motivational stories. As it seems, his storytelling has led him to a new and exciting career of writing mystery/thriller novels blended with a bit of ghostly paranormal activity. William discovered his gift of writing when he was writing the Gridiron News reports for his school.

Born and raised in Texas, William grew up in Dumas where there was never a dull moment. He now lives in the DFW area with his wife where they raised two children. He has always enjoyed outdoor activities and adventures as well as the paranormal. So being able to combine the two has created a unique twist on the typical mystery/thriller novel.